THE VET'S UNEXPECTED FAMILY

———

ALISON ROBERTS

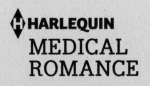

HARLEQUIN

MEDICAL ROMANCE

HARLEQUIN®
MEDICAL
ROMANCE™

Recycling programs
for this product may
not exist in your area.

ISBN-13: 978-1-335-40911-9

The Vet's Unexpected Family

Copyright © 2022 by Alison Roberts

This edition published by arrangement with Harlequin Books S.A.

For questions and comments about the quality of this book, please contact us at CustomerService@Harlequin.com.

Harlequin Enterprises ULC
22 Adelaide St. West, 41st Floor
Toronto, Ontario M5H 4E3, Canada
www.Harlequin.com

Printed in U.S.A.

Two Tails Animal Refuge

A second chance at life and love!

Welcome to Two Tails Animal Refuge in Australia's beautiful Blue Mountains! Vets Hazel and Kiara have one goal: to rescue and rehome vulnerable animals. The refuge staff work around the clock. So there's no time for Hazel and Kiara to think about love. Until a vet and a surgeon lead them to ask, "Is it time for my happily-ever-after?"

The Vet's Unexpected Family
By Alison Roberts

When a baby is abandoned at vet Hazel Davidson's Cogee Beach clinic, she's stunned to discover the newborn has been left in the care of her colleague Finn! The pair pull together to care for the baby, but could they become a real family?

A Rescue Dog to Heal Them
By Marion Lennox

All vet Kiara wants is enough money to keep her beloved Two Tails Animal Refuge afloat. But when she is paid to find a suitable rescue dog and help settle him with his new family, Kiara realizes she might have bitten off more than she can chew!

Both available now!

Dear Reader,

As my 100th romance novel, *The Vet's Unexpected Family* marks an astonishing milestone in my career, and this story is an appropriate celebration in many ways.

First, it's a Medical Romance, which reflects a world that has always been a huge part of my life. Finn and Hazel's story is set in the world of veterinary medicine and I love that my favorites—dogs and donkeys—make appearances.

The story is set in Australia and reminds me of the freedom and opportunities a career as a writer has given me. I've travelled widely for conferences and I'll never forget the magic of being able to live and work in the south of France.

And, last but not least, it's an absolute pleasure that such a significant book is part of a duo with my dear friend Marion Lennox, whom I've known for more than twenty years. It's a celebration of the wonderful friends who have come into my life through writing and who will be part of my chosen family forever.

I always hope that you enjoy reading my books as much as I love writing them but this time, I really hope it's something special.

With my love,

Alison Roberts xxx

Alison Roberts is a New Zealander, currently lucky enough to be living in the south of France. She is also lucky enough to write for the Harlequin Medical Romance line. A primary school teacher in a former life, she is now a qualified paramedic. She loves to travel and dance, drink champagne and spend time with her daughter and her friends. *The Vet's Unexpected Family* is Alison Roberts's 100th book.

Books by Alison Roberts

Harlequin Medical Romance

Twins Reunited on the Children's Ward

A Pup to Rescue Their Hearts
A Surgeon with a Secret

Royal Christmas at Seattle General

Falling for the Secret Prince

Medics, Sisters, Brides

Saved by Their Miracle Baby

The Paramedic's Unexpected Hero
Unlocking the Rebel's Heart
Stolen Nights with the Single Dad
Christmas Miracle at the Castle

Visit the Author Profile page
at Harlequin.com for more titles.

To each and every one of my readers because you make it possible for me to keep doing what I love.

And to Megan, my wonderful editor, who continues to inspire me to write the very best stories I can.

Thank you all so much. xxx

CHAPTER ONE

UH-OH...

About to walk into the waiting area of Coogee Beach Animal Hospital and summon her first patient for the afternoon clinic, Hazel Davidson stopped in her tracks. She took a step backwards, in fact, which put her behind the half-open door.

How had she forgotten it was Wednesday? One of the days when she had to be careful that she didn't end up being caught on camera by the television crew who had a weekly episode of *Call the Vet* to pre-record? Or rather, it *had* been *Call the Vet* in Series One. Now, halfway through Series Three it was more like *Call Dr Finn, Australia's Favourite Celebrity Vet—Not to Mention the Country's Most Eligible Bachelor*. And maybe that was why she'd forgotten to keep her head down today. Lately, there hadn't been as much filming happening in this veterinary clinic because the female fan base that gathered outside was starting to become a problem.

Maybe Hazel could catch the new receptionist's attention and get her to find the sixteen-week-old puppy waiting for its final health check and vaccination and bring it into the consulting room? That way, Hazel could stay completely below the radar, which was what she'd managed to do ever since that unfortunate appearance she'd been persuaded to make in Series One.

'I need you, Hazel,' Finn had said, and who could ignore a plea like that when it came with a smile that had always made her melt? *'It'll be fun,'* he'd said. But it hadn't ended up being fun at all, had it?

Kylie, the young receptionist, was watching Finn get some makeup brushed onto his face and then some hairspray on that floppy, sun-streaked hair, with the kind of dreamy expression that he probably inspired in all his biggest fans. It wasn't the first time that Hazel felt grateful her childhood had taught her the self-defence mechanism of hiding that kind of personal reaction—she would have looked like that herself in the early days of being around Dr Finn. Whatever... Kylie wasn't about to notice Hazel hovering behind the door.

She knew she should just go out there and find her patient herself. Except that one of the two cameramen had his camera secured on his shoulder and looked as though he could be filming already, even though Finn was deep in conversation with the person who seemed to be in charge, while he was getting the attention of the makeup artist, and there were three or four other people busy setting up equipment. She couldn't see an adorable puppy being cuddled anywhere, either, unless it was inside that solid, plastic pet carrier tucked in beside the wall display of dog toys and treats. The temptation to go back to her consulting room in the hope the television crew might have vanished by the time she came back was strong enough to really annoy her.

'Oh, for heaven's sake,' Hazel muttered. 'This is ridiculous.'

Lifting her chin, she pushed the door fully open and stepped into the waiting area, only to find that nobody even noticed her entrance. They were all turning in the opposite direction, at exactly the same time, as the automatic glass doors were sliding open and they could all hear someone calling for help.

'Oh, *no*...' Hazel pressed her fingers against her lips as she saw what they were watching. 'No, no, no...'

Someone was coming into the reception area at speed, holding what appeared to be a dog in their arms. A middle-aged woman, who was clearly distressed, her clothes streaked with blood.

'Please...can someone help? It just ran out in front of me...' The woman was sobbing. 'There was nothing I could do...'

Hazel was already halfway across the large room, oblivious to the fact that there were now two cameras trained on her. She reached the woman and took the dog as gently as possible from her arms, but it yelped in agony and Hazel could already see that its hind leg was deformed enough to be badly broken.

'This way...' Finn was guiding her towards his consulting room with a hand on her shoulder. The television crew scattered to create a clear path but, even as Hazel rushed past, she could feel their excitement. This was the kind of drama that couldn't be faked. It would have viewers on the edge of their seats and push their ratings sky high.

To his credit, however, Finn seemed just as disinterested as Hazel about who was watching. Their focus was entirely on a little black dog who'd just been hit by a car. A dog who was clearly shocked, whimpering in severe pain and breathing too fast as they laid him on the table as carefully as they could.

Hazel unhooked her stethoscope from around her neck but took a moment to lay her hand on the dog's head. He was mostly spaniel, by the look of those ears and the feel of his silky hair and he was no youngster, judging by that white muzzle.

'It's okay, pupper,' she said softly. 'We'll look after you...'

'No collar...' Finn noted. 'And he looks a bit under nourished. Could be a stray.' He ran his hands gently over the body of the dog, looking for the source of the bleeding as well as any obvious internal injuries. 'No life-threatening haemorrhage. Or not externally, anyway. There's a couple of lacerations that will need cleaning and suturing. Abdomen seems okay.'

'He's tachycardic.' Hazel held her stethoscope with one hand on the side of the dog's chest, where the beat was most prominent. She had the fingers of her other hand on the femoral artery. 'Pulse is weak. I'd say his blood pressure's too low.'

'I'll get an IV in.' Finn nodded. 'And put some fluids up.'

'I'll get some pain relief drawn up. We should get some oxygen on, as well.' Hazel looped her stethoscope back around her neck. 'We could do with another set of hands in here. Where's Anna?'

'I'm here.'

Hazel looked up to see their senior vet nurse, Anna, squeeze past a cameraman and a sound technician who was holding a fluffy microphone on a pole but she pushed aside the unwelcome realisation that she was being filmed. She was still too concerned for this dog's welfare to allow any distractions.

Finn picked up some clippers and Anna moved in without being asked to hold the dog's front leg still as a long patch was shaved to make it easy to find a vein.

Hazel opened drawers and swiftly found the IV supplies that Finn needed, putting them on the table beside him. A disinfectant wipe, cannula and plug, tape and bandage. Turning back to open the drug cabinet, she paused to unhook some tubing from the side of the anaesthetic trolley and turned on the oxygen cylinder. She put the end of the tube on the table near the dog's face.

'Flow-by oxygen at six litres a minute,' she

told Finn, who nodded his approval. 'Anna, can you keep the tube as close to his nose as you can while you're holding him?'

Finn slid the needle into a vein, inserted the cannula smoothly, capped it and unclipped the tourniquet in the space of seconds.

'Sorry, doggo,' he said. 'You'll feel better soon, I promise.'

Hazel had drawn up an opioid analgesic ready to inject by the time Finn had secured the IV firmly in place with tape and then a bandage on top. It seemed like it had been far too long but in reality it had only been a few minutes before they could all breathe a tentative sigh of relief. The injured dog was visibly relaxing as his pain level dropped, closing his eyes as the panting slowed so that he looked almost as if he was peacefully asleep. Now they could get on with the real business of stabilising their patient and potentially going ahead with emergency surgery to save its leg, if not its life.

Finn was drawing a blood sample from the IV line. He handed the syringe to Hazel. 'Can you run a CBC and electrolytes, please?' he asked. 'And do a catalyst chem seventeen. I want to know what the liver and kidney function is and whether it's safe to go ahead with anaesthesia if it's indicated. Which is very likely, going by that obvious fracture in his hind leg. That could well need some complex surgery.'

'Sure.'

But Hazel couldn't help a tiny head shake as she turned away to take the sample to the small room next to the X-ray suite that housed their state-of-the-art analysis technology that provided an in-house laboratory. While Hazel's reluctance to appear on the popular television show meant that they very rarely worked on the same patients these days, he knew that she knew exactly what blood tests were called for in an emergency situation like this and what the results could tell them. This was his television-speak, wasn't it? Demonstrating his expertise at the same time as explaining things for an audience that had no medical background?

'I could do that,' Anna said. 'And then make sure Theatre's good to go?'

Hazel shook her head. 'I've got a full clinic,' she said. 'The waiting room will be getting backed up.'

'No…' Finn glanced up swiftly from assessing the nasty leg fracture. 'Don't go. I need you, Hazel.'

There was no charmingly persuasive smile

to go with the plea this time but a direct glance like that from those dark eyes still never failed to melt something in that hidden space.

'Orthopaedic stuff like this is as much up your alley as mine,' he added. 'And I know just how talented you are.'

Anna was nodding her head to back him up. 'I've sorted the clinic,' she said, taking the blood sample from Hazel's hands. 'Nigel finished his surgery and he's taken your afternoon list. I could see that Finn needed you. And, even if people are waiting a bit longer, they understand when an emergency like this comes in.' She was halfway out the door, now, and Hazel had lost any opportunity to escape.

Part of her didn't want to, anyway. The dog's eyes were open again, although it was still lying calmly on the table and it was watching her with big, brown spaniel eyes. Finn might have tugged at her heartstrings by saying he needed her but this dog was telling her that his need was far more genuine. Desperate, even. And it felt like he was trusting her to stay close. She'd promised to look after him, hadn't she?

Hazel might have learned, over the last few years, to brush off any visceral response she still had to Finn's charisma but there was no way she could resist this dog. Her hand was already reaching out to stroke its ears again.

'We need X-rays,' Finn said. 'But I'm thinking that it could be a mission to save this leg, especially in an old fellow like this. Can you top up his pain relief and then I'll carry him next door so we can see exactly what we're dealing with?'

Hazel's thoughts were racing as she drew up some more medication. She had to stay now. To fight in this old dog's corner. What if it really was a stray and there was no one to pay what could end up being an exorbitant bill for medical treatment and rehab? What if the surgery was going to present such a challenge that would make it far easier to simply amputate the leg? Or, worst case scenario, would someone suggest that euthanasia was the sensible option?

Hazel closed her eyes as she drew in a slow breath, suddenly grateful that this emergency was being filmed. She didn't actually give a damn what people might say about her this time. She could ask the hard questions and make it impossible for easy decisions to be made too quickly. She could not only help to save this dog's life, she might get an opportunity to tell a lot of people about the passion in her life that had led to her becoming a vet in the first place and what she did in her time away from work. She could tell them about the Two Tails animal refuge up in the Blue Mountains and—who knew?—it might even lead to some badly needed financial support for the niche refuge run by Hazel's best friend, Kiara. The place that she headed for whenever she could, to do whatever she could to help.

Dealing with any fallout from a nationwide television appearance would be a small price to pay for being able to do something potentially more significant than simply turning up to help clean out dog runs or work alongside Kiara in her small veterinary practice.

Wouldn't it?

This was *great*.

Like the old days, when Hazel had first come to work at the Coogee Beach Animal Hospital. The days before *Call the Vet* became such a huge part of Finn's life, when almost every waking hour—and a few when he really should have been asleep—had been spent at the veterinary clinic he'd poured his heart and soul into building up after he'd come back home to Sydney.

He'd recognised the same passion in Hazel

when he'd chosen her for the new position of a permanent veterinary surgeon at the hospital and it had been the best decision he'd ever made. Her glowing references hadn't been exaggerated and they'd quickly formed a partnership in the operating theatre that was second to none. Finn hadn't realised quite how much he'd missed working with her, though, until they were deep into the intricate work of repairing the fracture on this emergency case that had come through the doors of the clinic this afternoon. He'd almost forgotten how clever her fingers were, how she could make thoughtful, balanced, major decisions in what seemed like the blink of an eye and…how much she *cared*.

He was watching her now, as she painstakingly picked out every tiny piece of shattered bone from the opening she had carefully created to expose this dog's serious leg fracture. Finn was happy to be Hazel's assistant as she tackled the delicate task of exposing and then repairing a complex fracture. Not only was he enjoying watching her skilled work, he knew that being this focused on the task at hand would make her forget she was being filmed.

Finn was very aware of what else the show's creative director would want, however, which was why this programme had become so astonishingly popular. He spoke quietly to the camera crew positioned on the other side of the clinic's main operating theatre to include the people who would, no doubt, be watching this procedure with fascination.

'So this is what we call a comminuted fracture,' he explained. 'Which means that the bone is broken in more than two places. Hazel's removing tiny shards of bone that could create problems for this dog down the track and then she'll decide the best method for stabilising the fracture so it can heal.' He adjusted the overhead light a fraction to put the brightest point above the hole in the sterile drapes covering their patient. He really wanted to draw Hazel into talking about what she was doing. If she enjoyed this, maybe she would consider being on the show on a regular basis.

'What are you thinking, Hazel?' he asked. 'Pins and cerclage wire? External fixation? Or plates and screws?'

'Plates and screws.' Hazel didn't look up from her work. 'We've got enough bone length both distal and proximal to the fracture to allow for the minimum three screws in each fragment. It's going to be the most stable solution.'

Finn smiled at the cameras. He knew the smile wouldn't be seen beneath his mask but it made a difference to the tone of his voice. It could make the audience feel as if they were sharing privileged information.

'As vets, we have what's called the "fifty/fifty" rule,' he said. 'You have to have at least fifty per cent of the ends of fractured bones in contact with each other and that fifty per cent reduction is the absolute minimum for bone healing to be possible. It has to be stable, too. Something like a splint or an external cast is the least stable method to reduce a fracture. Internal fixation using things like plates and screws is the most stable. Plus, it's the best choice for restoring length to a bone where there are lost pieces like the ones Hazel's removing.'

He paused, knowing that the camera would be zooming in on the stainless-steel kidney dish that Hazel was dropping the small bone fragments into. He was still doing too much talking, wasn't he? He needed to come up with a way of getting Hazel really engaged and hopefully wipe out the bad memories of the aftermath of appearing on the show for the first and only time.

Even now, well over a year later, it could make Finn cringe. Not that he'd been present when that unpleasant woman and her daughter had brought their Persian cat in for an appointment but he'd heard all about how unhappy they'd been when Hazel had arrived to welcome them. He'd read about it, in fact, when it got splashed over social media.

'Nah...' The woman had made sure everyone in the crowded waiting area could hear her. *'Like we said when we rang up, we want to see the TV vet. That's why we've come right across the city.'*

'Dr Davidson is one of the TV vets,' the receptionist had told them. *'She was on the show only last week.'*

'It's the guy we came to see. The good-looking one.'

The daughter had been even more blunt than her mother. *'That's right. We don't want the fat vet.'*

So Hazel was curvy? So what? As if that made a difference to her amazing skills and an awesome personality? Finn considered Hazel to be one of his closest friends and he'd been mortified on her behalf.

'It's the camera,' he'd told her. *'Everyone knows it adds a heap of weight. Good grief... I'm sure I look like the Hulk sometimes.'*

But Hazel had refused to talk about it. And now she was simply doing her job and not talking at all if she could help it. She might be doing an amazing job but even if viewers could recognise that, Finn wanted more. He wanted people to respect her. To like her—as much as he did.

'So...did you catch up on that guy who came into reception while we were doing the X-rays on this leg? The one who works at the Brazilian barbecue restaurant?'

Hazel shook her head. 'Have we got a two-point-five-millimetre drill bit on the trolley?'

'It's right here. Hiding beside the lag screws.'

'Thanks.'

'This guy heard about the accident and came in to talk to Kylie. He reckons he's been feeding this dog meat scraps for a week or so now. He's been trying to get close enough to catch it and take it to a refuge ever since but, while it'll take a bit of food, it always runs away if he tries to touch him.'

'Really?' This time, Hazel looked up. 'I forgot to ask when I got busy scrubbing in but did Anna check for a microchip, too?'

'There isn't one. We decided to go ahead with the surgery, though. As you know, we've got a fund to cover the occasional emergency like this.'

He could hear the way Hazel snatched in a quick breath. 'I know who can help after we discharge him. I've got a friend I've known for years—since vet school—and she runs the most amazing refuge centre up in the Blue Mountains.'

'Oh? Can they cater for a dog that's going to need intensive rehab? An old dog? Judging by his teeth and eyes and all that grey hair, this one could be well over twelve years old. Maybe fourteen or fifteen.'

'It can cater for any animal in an emergency but it specialises in rescuing cases exactly like this. Dogs or cats who are too old for most people to consider rehoming because they might not live that much longer and they often have expensive health care needs. The kind that vets get asked to put down all the time because their owners have died or gone into care themselves and there's nobody else to take on their pet.'

Finn was nodding. He'd had to face requests like that himself in the past and he'd hated it. It hadn't happened recently, though. Was that because he was more involved in his television work than the day-to-day work of a busy veterinary clinic or had Hazel been quietly rescuing these animals without him knowing about it?

He'd known how much she cared about her patients but his admiration for how much she cared for animals in general had just gone up several notches.

'And old dogs are *so* special,' she added, with a catch in her voice. 'I grew up with a dog who lived to be eighteen and he was…' Hazel hesitated and then seemed to change her mind about whatever she'd been planning to reveal. 'He was the reason I decided to become a vet,' she added. 'How could anyone even think of putting them down for the sake of convenience, or worse—dumping them when they can't possibly understand what they've done wrong because they *haven't* done anything wrong?'

Wow… Hazel had really come alive. She looked and sounded animated and her eyes were sparkling. The beeping of the heart monitor in the background made for a dramatic pause as she stopped speaking. Finn found himself wanting to know what it was that Hazel had decided not to say but he guessed that asking a question that touched personal ground could be the quickest way to make her back off again and he didn't want that to happen.

The conversation wasn't distracting her from the meticulous work she was doing, keeping the slippery stainless-steel plate she had already shaped to fit the bone in place as she drilled holes to take the screws that would secure it and Finn was experienced enough with this television stuff to know when he was onto a good thing. He could sense how clearly her passion would come across and how fast it would draw people in. Listening to this, the last thing anyone would think of would be to tag her with a derogatory physical descriptor like 'fat'. No…it would be words like 'passionate' and 'kind' and a 'totally awesome human' that would spring to mind. Maybe Hazel would get some feedback that would make her feel as good about herself as she had always deserved to feel. Finn was smiling beneath his mask again.

'Tell me about this refuge.'

'It's called Two Tails.' It sounded like Hazel was smiling as well. 'We came up with the name together. Because, you know—you can be as happy as a dog with two tails?'

'It's a great name.'

'It's two tales, as well. As in stories? Because they have a sad story that brings them into the refuge and a happy story in the end, or that's what we do our best to achieve, anyway.'

'We…?'

'I help out whenever I can. That's why I drive a dodgy old van instead of a proper car.'

'It's hardly a dodgy old van. It's a vintage Morris Minor delivery van.' He gave one of his trademark grins directly to camera, as if he were talking confidentially to someone who was watching the programme. 'Bright red. Very cute.'

Hazel snorted. 'Whatever. What matters is that I can fit a couple of crates in the back and I don't care if I have to cross the city to pick up a dog or cat from a vet clinic or refuge after work or if the phone goes in the middle of the night because there's an animal in distress somewhere. Not that I can do everything. We got a call about a donkey who has to be urgently rehomed because it hasn't had its feet trimmed in so long it can't walk but I couldn't have fitted her in the van and, anyway, there isn't paddock space at the refuge.'

Finn made a sympathetic sound but didn't want to interrupt. He'd never heard Hazel so eager to talk about something that was part of her private life.

'I totally love the refuge,' she added. 'And I have the greatest admiration for what Kiara does. Some of the stories are heartbreaking but she does her absolute best every single time. Even now, when it's getting so much harder.'

'In what way is it getting harder?'

'Oh, you know…' Hazel had put the last screw in and was examining the bone and surrounding tissue before starting to close up the wound. 'Financial stuff. It's never cheap looking after animals, especially if they've got underlying health issues and, sadly, some of them come back or even end up staying at the refuge for the rest of their lives.' She looked up from her work to let her gaze rest on that sleeping face with the grey muzzle. 'I would hate that to happen to this old boy. I'd take him myself, in a heartbeat, if I could but I live in a basement bedsit with too many stairs. If he does end up at Two Tails, though, I'll be there every day.'

Finn made a mental note to talk to the show's producer. They could put the details for Two Tails up as a subtitle or at the end of this episode, directing people to where they could make a donation, perhaps. Not that it would be on screen for a while, yet, but it could help in the long run. He'd tell

Hazel about the plan later. If nothing else, it would ensure that she wouldn't back out of letting herself appear on screen and Finn wanted this episode to go to air. He had a good feeling about contributing to a rescue case like this and for one of his colleagues to be passionately directing public attention to the welfare of a section of the pet population that many people probably hadn't considered an issue.

He also had a good feeling about how successful this surgery would be. He leaned closer to look at the result as Hazel irrigated the wound and swabbed it dry.

'You've done an amazing job plating that,' he told Hazel. 'I can't even see the fracture lines.'

'We just need to close up and splint this leg and then deal with the other lacerations. I'd like to get him out of anaesthesia as soon as we can.'

Finn reached for some sutures. 'He needs a name. We can't just put "Old Dog" on his crate, can we?'

'Ben.' Hazel's suggestion was so quick, Finn knew it was significant.

'Was that the name of your dog?' he asked quietly. 'The one you grew up with?'

Hazel didn't look up. 'Yeah…he was black,

too.' Her tone was dismissive enough to signal that this topic of conversation was terminated. 'Now…let's get this periosteum wrapped back over the bone.'

It was well over an hour later when Ben the old, black dog was finally tucked up amongst soft blankets in the hospital ward, under the care of an expert vet night nurse who was being briefed by Anna. The television crew was packing up their gear, the waiting room had emptied of patients and their owners, Kylie the receptionist was getting ready to head home and Hazel had changed out of her scrubs and into street clothes.

'I'm just going to grab something to eat and I'll be back,' she told Finn. 'I'm going to stay and keep an eye on Ben for a while.'

Finn nodded. He was with the show's producer and they were both peering at the monitor attached to one of the huge cameras.

'That's a great shot, Jude,' he said. 'I should do a voice over to explain what's happening but I'd hate to cut anything Hazel's saying about the refuge. That's gold, isn't it?'

'I like it,' the producer agreed. 'Might be worth thinking about following up with a visit out there. It's a cute name, isn't it? Two Tails?'

It didn't matter that Hazel had missed lunch. Any urgent need to find something to eat had just evaporated. *This* was exciting. It might even be a turning point for the refuge. She turned back well before the automatic doors were triggered to open, searching for the right words that might encourage the idea of Finn and the crew visiting the refuge, when something stopped her saying anything at all.

A sound that was so completely unexpected in a waiting area that was empty of any patients, it was shocking. It was a demanding kind of sound, like the yowl of a hungry Siamese cat. Hazel wasn't the only person bewildered by the noise.

'What on earth was that?' Finn asked. 'There's no one there.'

Hazel was looking in the direction the sound had come from, over by the display of toys and treats for dogs and cats. Oddly, there was a pet carrier on the floor, which didn't match the kind that the clinic had for sale and Hazel realised she'd seen that carrier before—when the area had been crowded with people waiting for the afternoon clinic to start. Just before the chaos of the emergency had kicked off.

'Someone must have forgotten their pet,'

Hazel said. 'It wouldn't be the first time. They'll get home and panic when the carrier's not in the back of the car.'

Shaking her head, she walked over to the carrier and crouched down to peer through the wire door on the front. Or rather, try to peer past a small sheet of paper that had been taped to the door. She read the words on the paper but they made no sense. So she opened the door and stared inside, as the cry came again. Louder this time.

'Oh, my God…' she breathed. 'It's a *baby*…'

'No way…' Finn was staring across the waiting area. 'It can't be…'

'It *is*. There's a note, here, too.'

Hazel could see the cameraman and the show producer exchanging a meaningful glance as she peeled the paper from the wire door. The camera got swung back into position on the man's shoulder. There was more drama happening at the Coogee Beach Animal Hospital and they didn't want to miss a moment of it.

'What does the note say?'

Hazel hesitated. Finn might not want to make this public. The way his long strides were eating up the space between them, there was no time to keep this completely private but at least she could show him the note rather than reading it aloud. She could also watch the colour drain out of his face as he read it.

To Dr Finn
You look after animals all the time on your show.
So you can look after this kid.
She's yours.

CHAPTER TWO

THE HUFF OF sound that came from Finn was beyond incredulous.

'She's mine? Someone's trying to give me a *kid*? What is this—some kind of joke?' He swung round to face a camera pointing directly at him. 'It is, isn't it? A prank? Is it someone's birthday or have I missed a milestone for the show or something?'

'I don't think they're trying to give you someone else's child,' Hazel said quietly. 'I think this note suggests that she's already yours.' The muscles in her face felt oddly tense. 'That maybe you're the father?'

Nobody else was saying anything, except for the baby who let out its loudest wail yet. Anna had walked into the waiting area as Hazel was speaking but was now frozen to the spot. Kylie was staring at him with her mouth open. Jude, the show's producer, had raised her eyebrows so high they'd vanished under her short fringe. The guy with the camera on his shoulder looked as if he could be smirking.

'What…?' Finn was looking even more gobsmacked than he had when he'd finished reading the note. 'You can't possibly believe this could be *true*…?'

His head was turning and Hazel knew he was about to catch her gaze. That he would be quite sure she would back him up a hundred per cent—the way she always did. And she wanted to be there for him. To hold his gaze and let him know that she'd always be there for him but, instead, for some reason, she found herself ducking her head the nanosecond before he could make eye contact and reaching into the pet carrier to carefully extract the baby.

Goodness knew how she had stayed asleep for so long but this infant definitely needed attention now. Her bottom felt distinctly damp through its towelling stretch suit so Hazel pulled a fuzzy blanket, printed with yellow ducks, out as well, to wrap around the damp patch. She got to her feet with the small bundle firmly clutched against her chest and, by some miracle, the human contact made the baby happy enough to stop crying. She was looking up at Hazel with wide open dark eyes as she looked down and, oh, boy...this wasn't a squeeze on her heart in response to the most adorable baby she'd ever seen, it was more like a squeeze on her ovaries that was so fierce it really hurt.

She'd always adored animals, dogs in particular—and Ben most of all and for ever—because of the unconditional and unlimited love they offered so willingly but oh, my... there was an unfamiliar yearning deep inside her belly right now that suggested a baby could fill an even bigger gap in your life. *Her* life, anyway.

'Oh...you're *gorgeous*...' Hazel had to touch the longest, darkest hair she'd ever seen on a baby. It was also the softest. 'I've never seen a baby with actual curls like this. And look at those eyelashes...'

Anna had recovered the ability to move and she was by Hazel's side in a heartbeat, also ready to coo over the baby.

'It must be a girl. Nobody would put a boy in a pink, unicorn onesie would they?'

'It is a girl,' Hazel told her. 'The note referred to her as "she".'

Finn made an exasperated sound. He screwed up the note and threw it away. He glared at the cameraman. 'You can stop filming right now, mate. This isn't funny. For heaven's sake, everyone knows I've been in a relationship with Shannon Summers for at least a *year.*'

Hazel bit her lip. Surely everyone also knew it was an on-again, off-again kind of arrangement? She couldn't be the only one to think there was something phoney about his relationship with such a popular social media star that hooking up had made them Australia's most talked about IT couple? Everyone would, no doubt, suspect there were limitless women waiting in the wings for the celebrity TV vet to be ready to take another break or move on and many of them would be tall, super-skinny blondes like Shannon.

Like all the women he'd dated over the first year or so when Hazel came to work here, for that matter. The kind of women that had let her know instantly there was no point even thinking about ever being invited to step out of a 'friend and/or colleague' zone for Finn, even if his charm often seemed to border on flirting with those meaningful glances and *that* smile. Hazel knew that was just part of his charisma and it was like water off a duck's back for her now.

'Maybe we should call the police,' Jude suggested. 'Abandoning a baby has got to be against the law. It's certainly headline news, that's for sure.' Her gaze slid sideways towards her cameraman.

'Uh, uh…' Finn had seen the look. 'This is not getting anywhere near a news broadcast. Whoever's done this must be after the publicity for some reason. It's the sort of thing that happens to celebrities all the time.'

'I'm not sure about that,' Hazel murmured. 'Paternity claims, maybe, but actually leaving your baby where the father is going to be forced to take care of it? Not so much…'

'I'm *not* the father.' Finn had such a haunted look in his eyes that Hazel knew he was telling the truth.

'You could get a DNA test done,' Jude suggested. 'I've got a friend who works in a lab that does them. I believe it's possible to get an urgent result through in forty-eight hours or so. Want me to give them a call?'

'And have you filming it?' Finn shook his head. 'I'll pass on that one, thanks. There's no point doing it anyway. The chance of me being this baby's father is about the same as a snowball's chance in hell. You may as well all go home.'

'I wonder if there's anything else in here.' Anna crouched to examine the carrier. 'Yeah, look…there's a bottle and some formula at the back. And a few nappies.'

'She needs one of those.' Hazel nodded. 'I'll change her if you want to make up a bottle.'

'Okay.' But Anna was frowning as she looked up. 'What else did the note say, apart from her being a girl?'

Hazel glanced at Finn who was still looking anguished. She looked at Jude and her crew who were looking very reluctant to leave this new drama unfolding in front of them. Kylie helpfully dived for the screwed-up ball of paper and unfolded it to hand to Anna.

'Wait,' Hazel ordered. 'Let me see that?' Both she and Finn had only seen the note scrawled in dark ink on one side of the paper. Now she could see there was something written on the other side.

'Elena Ferrari,' she read aloud as the baby started crying again. 'Date of birth twenty-ninth of August…so that makes the baby…'

'About six weeks old,' Anna supplied. 'And obviously hungry… I'm going to make up that bottle.' She reached into the carrier to take the items she needed.

'Ferrari…?' Finn was frowning. '*Elena* Ferrari?'

'Maybe someone knows what sort of car

you drive.' The suggestion came from the crew's sound technician.

'He drives a Porsche,' the cameraman said. 'Black. Late model. Better than a Ferrari if you ask me.'

'It's an odd name.' Jude sounded thoughtful. 'Italian, but not that common in Australia, I wouldn't have thought.'

Hazel was watching Finn. And she couldn't help herself—she wanted to get involved. To try and help, somehow. Good grief, the urge to touch him was astonishingly strong. Not just the touch of a friend, either. She wanted to wrap her arms around Finn and hold him tightly. Luckily, the urge was easy to dismiss thanks to the baby she was holding.

'Do you recognise the name?' she asked.

'I had a friend at high school,' he said slowly. And *her* name was Elena Ferrari.' He rubbed the back of his neck. 'Weird co-incidence, huh?'

'Was she a close friend?' Hazel couldn't agree with his assumption. 'A *girl*friend?'

She could see the answer to that query in the way Finn's face softened, even before his single, slow affirmatory nod. The misty look that had darkened his eyes to a real, deep sea kind of blue made her think that Elena must have been someone rather special. A first love, perhaps?

Lucky girl...

But that odd frisson of something like envy was fading rapidly because there was a part of Hazel's brain that was doing a bit of rapid calculation, having decided that there was more to this than coincidence. James Finlay was thirty-six years old. He would have been about seventeen towards the end of high school. If the mother of this baby was also that young, then...

Then...

'Oh, my God, Finn,' Hazel whispered. 'This doesn't have to be your daughter to be yours, does it? Has it occurred to you that this could be your *grand*daughter?'

Okay.

That did it.

Finn hadn't got to where he was in life without being able to take charge of a tricky situation and get himself out of trouble. Not that he'd ever expected to find himself in a pickle quite like this, of course, but the absurdity of even the idea that he could have a grandchild made it imperative that this got nipped in the bud. *Now*.

'Anna, can you please make up some formula for the baby? Kylie… I know you're heading home but could you please do a supermarket run first and get a few supplies that we might need in the next hour or so?' He offered her the most persuasive smile he could summon and it seemed to work.

'Like what?'

'Another pack of nappies, more formula. Anything else that looks useful in the baby aisle.' He handed her a card from his wallet. 'Use the practice account.' He shifted his gaze as the automatic doors opened for Kylie to exit. 'The rest of you can go home, thanks. I'll be getting in touch with the police or Social Services or whoever deals with this kind of thing and we'll have it sorted in no time. Oh…and, Jude? I might get the name of that friend of yours, after all. The one who works with DNA testing? Just in case.'

Hazel was walking towards him and, to his horror, Finn got the distinct impression that she might be planning to hand over the baby. Did she think he'd included her in the people he had just told to go home?

'You can't go home, Hazel.' He spoke firmly so that his message was completely clear but the way her eyebrows shot up made her look astonished. Appalled, even?

'I need you,' he added. He tried that smile

again—the one that had worked so well on Kylie—but it seemed to have lost its magic. 'Please?' He simply mouthed the plea but he held her gaze and tried to add whatever else it might take because he really *did* need her.

I know I sound like I'm in control, but I'm not... I'm a bit lost, to be honest...and, out of all my friends, you're the one I trust the most...

Maybe Hazel was a bit telepathic. Or maybe she was just confirming what he already knew—that she was the nicest person in the world.

'I'm just going into the consulting room,' she said, calmly. She held up the nappy in her hand. 'I need a flat surface and some wipes.'

Finn stayed in the waiting area, grateful for the empty space while he took several deep breaths and tried to decide who he needed to call first. The police? His agent? His solicitor? Or Shannon—to warn her that something was developing that she might not want to use to update her status? Kylie came back before he'd made that decision with what looked like a pack of nappies big enough to last a month under one arm and a bag of more supplies in her other hand.

'I have to go now,' she said. 'I don't want to miss my bus.'

She left as Anna came back with a bottle of warm formula at the same time as Hazel returned with the baby who didn't appear to appreciate having clean pants. It was howling the roof down. Anna handed Finn the bottle of milk.

'I need to get back into the ward and check on our post-op cases. Including your Ben.'

'Oh...'

Hazel was biting her lip. She clearly wanted to go and see the old dog, too, but that would mean that Finn would be left with the baby. He didn't give her a chance to move first. He handed her the bottle.

'Come and sit down,' he said. 'You'll be much more comfortable.'

'I'll look after Ben,' Anna promised. 'He'll probably just sleep for the rest of the night, anyway.'

'But...'

'The police will need to talk to you,' Finn added. 'You're the one who found the kid, after all. You might be able to remember something else?'

Hazel sank down on one of the padded benches. The pet carrier that had been the cause of this new crisis was still nearby. Empty now, with its wire door hanging open. A bomb that had already been detonated.

'It might have fingerprints on it,' he said hopefully. 'We can find the mother.'

'Mmm…' Hazel sounded dubious but she was focused on getting the baby to accept the teat of the bottle. She adjusted her hold and made soothing sounds but it took another attempt or two before the red-faced, miserable infant latched on and then started furiously sucking. It looked like it was glaring up at Hazel.

'Poor thing,' Hazel murmured. 'You were starving, weren't you, Ellie?'

Finn almost winced at the shortened form of a name that echoed in his memory banks. No…he wasn't going to think about the Ellie he remembered. About the way his life had been so devastatingly derailed.

'What did you mean,' he demanded, 'by "mmm"? You don't think the mother's going to be found?'

'That wasn't what I was thinking about. But I'm sure she'll be found if she wants to be found.'

'What's that supposed to mean?'

'She might be really young and having trouble coping. She might need a bit of time. This could be a cry for help—maybe to the only family member she, or possibly *he*, can approach.'

'I'm *not* a family member.' But it was beginning to feel like he could well be clutching at a straw, here.

'Think about it, Finn,' Hazel said. 'A baby gets left for you to find. A baby who has the same name as a girl you were in a relationship with, what...seventeen, eighteen years ago? Can you be absolutely sure the first Elena Ferrari that you knew didn't get pregnant?'

'I wouldn't know.' The words came out curtly. Good grief...he'd thought he'd left that hurt behind nearly two decades ago. 'She left school before I did. I never heard from her again.'

'Mmm...'

Hazel was making that infuriating sound again—as if he was being a bit dense, not joining the dots. And, okay...being a pregnant, unmarried teenager could be the reason she'd left school so abruptly, especially with an already less than ideal home situation but...

But the enormity of considering that this could be true—that he'd simply skipped fatherhood to become a *grandfather*?

No. No, no, no...

Baby Ellie had certainly been hungry. As her little tummy filled she was sinking into Hazel's arms, feeling both limper and heavier. Her eyelids were getting heavier as well, and she was having trouble keeping them open. Hazel had bottle fed orphaned kittens or puppies and even a kangaroo joey or two in her time but, somehow, she'd got to be thirty-two years old and had never fed a human baby. If it was like this with a bottle, it was mindboggling to imagine that it could be even more intense to be breastfeeding. She could feel emotions stirring that were big enough to become overwhelming and Hazel was blinking them away when she became aware of something else.

Finn was watching her.

Really watching her. Not just observing her, as he'd been doing when he was watching her operate on Ben's fractured leg. Or the way he'd look when he was teasing her, if they were out in a crowd having 'after work' drinks or celebrating something, by giving her those appreciative glances as they clinked glasses as a toast or laughed at someone's joke. Hazel knew, when she looked up, that she wouldn't see a persuasively raised eyebrow or lopsided smile on his face and it was in that moment she suddenly realised that a lot of James Finlay's life was a disguise. Some form of protection?

For different reasons, no doubt, Finn was grappling with some overwhelming emotions himself, wasn't he?

And there was a connection here, between them. Because he was watching her holding this baby and it felt like he was seeing her—really *seeing* her, as a person and not a colleague or a friend or inside any other people box he might have a label on—for possibly the first time ever.

'What if it's true?' His words were no more than a whisper. 'It would destroy my image. My career, probably. My life, possibly.'

'You never know,' Hazel said. 'It could turn out to be the best thing that's ever happened to you.'

Finn gave one of those incredulous huffs again. 'What am I going to do? Shall I call Social Services? Do you think they have an emergency refuge for babies like we do for dogs or kangaroos or whatever?'

Hazel could feel her hold on baby Ellie tighten just a fraction. 'What if it is true?' She tried to keep her tone casual. 'Don't you think that abandoning your grandchild to an emergency foster home might be worse for your image?' Then she frowned. 'Have you not called someone already?'

Finn shook his head. He looked beyond miserable. 'I can't think what the best thing to do is. How I'm going to keep the media from getting hold of this. It's already out there, isn't it? Jude might be looking out for me, but there's plenty of other people in that crew who'll have friends in the industry who'd love a scoop like this.'

Okay… The emotions Hazel could feel surfacing now weren't anything like the ones that could have brought tears to her eyes. She was feeling rather fiercely protective of this baby she was holding. She was also feeling more than a little disappointed in how superficial Finn was making himself sound. So what if the life and persona he'd built were some form of protection? This was…well, it was unacceptable, that was what it was.

'No wonder you and Shannon Summers are so perfect for each other,' she found herself saying aloud. 'You both believe that what other people think—preferably the millions of people who follow you on social media— is way more important than anything else, don't you?'

Finn blinked at her. He'd been expecting support, not an attack. And this was not the time to be letting stuff out that had prob-

ably been building for a very long time—
ever since Hazel had realised she might have
fallen in love with Finn—but it felt like a pin
had been pulled from a grenade and there
was no stopping it now.

'You're superficial,' she snapped. 'Both
of you. You skate through life on your good
looks and wealth and…you're fake. It's all
fake. All that celebrity and social media crap.
This…' Hazel looked down at the baby who
had fallen deeply asleep now, the teat of the
bottle loose in her mouth. 'This is real. *This*
is what matters.'

She stood up, pressing the bundle of baby
against Finn's chest, knowing that he would
instinctively bring his arms up to protect it.

'Meet Ellie,' she finished. 'You might not
believe this, but I think showing you care
about a baby who's very likely to be your
granddaughter will do a lot of good for your
image. And your career. And, most of all,
for your life.'

She turned her back on him, intending to
walk away to go and see how Ben the black
dog was doing but she suddenly needed to
get a lot further away from Finn than that.
Completely away from this clinic, in fact,
which made her swerve towards the auto-

matic doors. The nurse on duty in their post-op ward would be taking excellent care of Ben and she could text Hazel at any time if she had concerns. And Anna was right—with the painkillers Ben was receiving along with the IV fluids, he was more than likely to be comfortably asleep all night.

She couldn't go home though. How awful would it be to sit in that lonely little apartment in the wake of what was turning into the worst day of her life, what with the horror of seeing Ben being rushed into the clinic like that, finding Ellie and stirring such strong feelings about motherhood that she hadn't been aware she had and…and seeing Finn with the filter that was a mix of physical attraction and a much deeper level of affection well and truly peeled off? She'd been suppressing a one-sided attraction ever since the first day she'd met this man so was this the first occasion that she was seeing the *real* James Finlay? Someone who was so focused on his celebrity status and popularity that he was totally missing even some compassion for a helpless baby who'd been abandoned?

There was only one place she could go that might turn her day around.

Two Tails.

And the sooner she was there, with her own reality of true friendship and doing some good in a world that all too often lacked compassion these days, the better.

CHAPTER THREE

THE BLUE MOUNTAINS covered thousands of square miles of rugged country west of Sydney, Australia and they had earned their name because, from a distance, the eucalyptus and gum trees that blanketed the area created a haze with a distinctly blue tinge. A popular tourist destination, the mountains were known for forests and sandstone cliffs, canyons and waterfalls, underground caves, hundreds of miles of walking tracks and a rich, indigenous history and culture to explore.

Even as preoccupied as she was with the emotional overload she was escaping, Hazel couldn't miss the spectacular haze of the mountains this evening, accentuated by the sun beginning to set behind them and she could feel some of her stress already evaporating as she drew in a long slow breath and then let it out in a sigh. She would feel even better when she took the turn off to the small town of Birralong that was isolated enough to have never become part of the Blue Mountain tourist trail, despite being only an hour or so from central Sydney.

She was longing to be there—sitting on the shady wide veranda of the tumbledown old house her best friend Kiara had inherited from her grandmother on the outskirts of Birralong, with its rambling garden and forest surroundings—because Hazel knew it would be the perfect place to unpick one of the worst days she could remember in a very long time. Not that she could have a glass of wine tonight, because she intended to get back to work later and check on Ben, but maybe she and Kiara could even find something kind of funny about her car crash of an afternoon. Dr Finn's fall from stardom because his love life had finally caught up with him, perhaps?

No. Hazel might be seeing her boss in a disappointing new light but she'd never take pleasure in bad things happening to anyone, let alone someone she cared about as much as she cared about Finn. Her sigh this time wasn't one of relief. It was more like satisfaction that she wasn't doing the wrong thing trekking right out of the city when it hadn't

been planned for today. It certainly wasn't
going to make her day any worse to be with a
person who was so special in her life and in a
place that had captured her heart to the point
of feeling like a real home years ago now.

Not that she would ever be able to afford to
live out here. It was enough of a struggle for
Kiara to make ends meet despite having been
lucky enough to have been gifted a property.
The rambling garden around Kiara's cottage,
with just enough land cleared in the forest to
provide space for the refuge and her small
veterinary clinic, had to be worth a fortune
with it being within such easy commuting
distance from Sydney.

It was priceless as far as Hazel was concerned, anyway, and she couldn't wait to get
there. She could already feel her mood lifting as she slowed her speed to drive through
central Birralong but then she saw something
on the side of the road near a bus stop. Something that made her hit the brakes hard on
her beloved van, Morrie.

It was a dog.

Lying so still it could be dead but, even if
it *was* dead, she couldn't leave it here. Her
heart heavy, Hazel opened the back of her
van. She had warm blankets in here, along
with the crates. There was a powerful torch

for an emergency at night, a shovel and crow-bar in case of entrapment and thick gloves that could offer protection from a frightened or aggressive animal. She put the gloves on and took a blanket.

'What's happened?' A man had crossed the street and was approaching as Hazel crouched on the road and covered the dog's body with the blanket. 'Did it get hit by a car?'

Two dogs hit by cars in the space of one afternoon would be much less of a coincidence than, say…a baby that just happened to have been given the same name as an old girlfriend, but Hazel was shaking her head.

'I don't think so. There's no obvious sign of external injury. It may have been abandoned because it was sick and someone couldn't afford to take it to a vet.'

'Unbelievable. At least it's not dead. I can see it's breathing.'

Hazel blinked. But the man was right. The blanket over the dog was moving. She pulled it back and the man sucked in his breath.

'Crikey…look at the way his bones are sticking out.'

'Mmm.' Hazel had no words to find. She was looking at one of the worst cases of animal abuse she'd ever seen. A skeletal, black and white female dog, possibly a border collie but it was hard to tell with that matted hair and those infected sores. But she *was* breathing and her eyes were half open.

'There's a vet not far away,' the Birralong resident told her. 'At the refuge up the road.'

'I know. That's actually where I'm heading.' And it wouldn't be the first time that a sick or injured animal had been left close enough to the refuge to be easily found.

'Oh…that's good, then.' The man hesitated for only a moment. 'I can help you put it in your van, if you like.'

Hazel simply nodded. She was starting to feel a bit numb, to be honest. This was the last thing she needed to deal with right now.

The man waited until she'd closed Morrie's back door, ready to transport her blanket-wrapped patient. 'Doesn't look good, does it?'

'No. But thanks for your help.'

'I've heard she's good—the vet up at the refuge. She should be able to help.'

'I hope so.' Hazel got into her driver's seat. She wasn't sure anyone would be able to help this poor dog but at least she and Kiara could give her a more comfortable place to die than on the side of a road.

It was just as well it wasn't far to Two

Tails because Hazel had tears rolling down her face by the time she parked the van and gently carried the dog towards the front yard of the house, knowing that it was unlikely that Kiara would be in the clinic building this late in the day.

'Kiara?' Her voice sounded as strangled as she was feeling inside. 'Kiara? Where are you?'

'In the pens. Hang on, I'm coming…'

'I found her on the side of the road near the bus stop in Birralong,' Hazel told her friend as soon as she appeared. 'She's…oh, Kiara… this is just awful…'

Kiara crouched beside her, taking in every horrible detail that Hazel had already seen but it was still like seeing it all over again through her eyes and…it was too much. She had to turn away as she blinked back tears. Looking back, she saw Kiara cradling the dog's head in her hands as she looked at it the same way she had looked at Ben only hours ago. It was enough to break her heart all over again but someone had to be practical, even though she hated that it had to be her.

'Can we even do anything to help her?' Hazel asked quietly. 'It might be kinder to…' She couldn't bring herself to say the words and she had tears flowing again. 'On top of everything else that's happened today… I don't think I can bear it.'

Kiara flashed her a glance that let Hazel know she wanted to hear about what else had happened today, but not yet. They had something far more urgent to deal with.

'She's only young,' Kiara said. 'Maybe…'

'Oh, Kiara…look at her. She's been so abused that, even if we did manage to save her life, how scarred is she going to be? Physically and emotionally? Then there's the cost. Who's going to pay? We both know that sometimes the kindest thing to do is…is to let them go. We can make sure she's not in any pain.'

'We're going to do more than that.' Kiara hadn't looked away from the dog. 'Let's get her into the surgery.' Finally, she looked up, meeting Hazel's gaze square on. 'I know it doesn't make sense and we can't afford to take on a case like this but, dammit, Hazel, we set up Two Tails for a reason. If I'm going to end up bankrupt, then I'll go down doing what I do to the end.'

Maybe fighting talk was exactly what Hazel needed to hear. A reminder that when the going got tough was when the tough got going. Kiara was tough. And Hazel knew she was tough as well, deep down. She'd got back up after repeated knocks over the years, hadn't she? To be fighting on the same side as someone else, with the same goal and the encouragement and support they could give each other to succeed, was a gift that had come late in life for Hazel.

Meeting Kiara at vet school had given her the kind of friendship she'd only dreamed of having throughout her childhood and adolescence. The kind of friendship that was based on the things that mattered in life, like who you really were and not what you looked like. Things like love and loyalty and compassion. The kind of friendship that could give you the strength to tackle challenges even if they looked impossible.

They could do this.

What followed was a far more intense and difficult session treating a dog than this afternoon's efforts had been. Even giving enough sedation to allow them to work on the collie was precarious due to how close to death she was.

Because Kiara and Hazel were very used to working together and knew exactly what they were doing, they could distract themselves from unpleasant tasks, like removing matted hair and cleaning nasty lesions, by talking about other things, even if they were also disheartening.

'Have you any idea how you might cover costs?' Hazel asked at one point.

'Why bother?' Kiara shook her head. 'What's another debt among so many? Two Tails is doomed to close anyway.'

'What? No...'

'I got a quote to repair the termite damage and it's...well, it's impossible. Even if I mortgaged the property to find the money, I wouldn't be able to meet the repayments.'

'You can't close.' The thought was horrible. 'What if you charged more?'

'How? By taking in more dogs and selling them to the highest bidder? That's not how we do things.'

'Publicity, then? I took part in an episode of *Call the Vet* that was being filmed today and I talked about Two Tails. The show's producer is interested in coming out here and doing an episode and, with a bit of luck, it could lead to donations.'

'Wait a minute...' Kiara seemed to be ignoring a potential solution to the money problems. 'I thought you swore over your dead body that you'd never appear in that programme again?'

'I did. But there was a hit and run outside the clinic.' Hazel shrugged. 'I guess it comes with the territory but this one got to me. A gorgeous, old black spaniel who's apparently a stray.' Hazel looked away from Kiara's gaze. 'He needed surgery to plate a tibial fracture. Finn thought he must be about fourteen or fifteen years old. He also needed a name, so I called him Ben.'

'Ben? Wasn't that your first ever dog?'

'Yeah.'

'So we're both suckers for dogs.'

'I guess we are.'

They worked in silence for a minute. Kiara knew about Ben. How her old dog's company had been the only friendship Hazel could count on as she got bullied viciously throughout her school years and how it had given her the ambition to become a vet. How devastating it had been to lose him even though he'd lived to such a grand old age.

Kiara had also guessed long ago that Hazel had feelings for Finn that didn't mesh with simply being a friend or colleague.

'Well, then...' It was a slightly hesitant push. 'Was that what made it a bad day for you? Having to work with Finn? Or did Ben not make it?'

Hazel shook her head. 'Ben's doing well as far as I know. I'll go and check on him when

I'm done here.' She hesitated for a heartbeat. 'It's Finn who's not doing so well. A baby got left in the waiting room with a note that said it was his.'

'No...' Kiara was thoroughly distracted as she continued working. 'Tell me...'

So Hazel told her all about finding baby Ellie. And all about how disappointed she'd been in Finn's reaction.

'To be fair,' Kiara mused, 'it would be a bit of a shock to find out that you're a grand-father when you are out there as—what was it? Australia's most eligible bachelor?'

'Doesn't excuse him being so shallow.'

'His girlfriend won't be happy. Isn't she the one who makes her living by kneeling on beaches with her hands behind her head and then getting the photos touched up to provide unachievable body goals for other women?'

Hazel had to laugh. 'Yep. She's an influencer.' She straightened up to ease the ache in her back from bending over for so long. 'I'm just going to get a glass of water.'

She checked her phone that was lying on the bench beside the sink. She'd missed hearing the alert for a text message, which gave her a beat of panic that Ben's condition had deteriorated but the message wasn't from the night nurse at the hospital. It wasn't from Anna, either. It was from Finn.

Where are you? The message said. Can you please call me?

Hazel was not ready to communicate with Finn again yet. She could still hear the echo of her own voice, telling him he was fake and that celebrity status and money were more important to him than something that really mattered. Instead of responding to the message, she pulled on a fresh pair of gloves to continue the work on the collie. They were getting close enough to see the end point of this first attempt to rescue her and, while shaving more and more of the matted hair away wasn't doing anything to make the dog look more attractive, it still felt positive. Hazel just wished that Kiara would start looking a bit happier.

'The world's gone a bit mad,' she told Hazel. 'People have enough stress to deal with these days without people like influencers making it worse.'

'Who did you have in mind?'

'I had my own share of drama today, too. With a man who's got major issues of his own and, on top of that, he's now got responsibility for a little girl—his niece—who's traumatised after her mother took her own life. His sister came to see me the other day and asked if I'd provide a dog for them. She seemed to think a dog would solve all their problems and she offered me pretty much enough money to sort out the termites if I could organise it.'

'Really?' Hazel paused before turning on the clippers again. 'That sounds too good to be true.'

'The amount she offered me was ridiculous,' Kiara finished. 'And I don't even have a dog suitable for a child.'

'How about this one?' Hazel suggested.

Kiara had also paused. She was staring at her. 'Are you out of your mind?'

'Maybe. But it sounds as if there are two wounded souls that need help. Why not make it three?'

'Hazel, that's ridiculous.'

'You'll need to find a home for her, even if you are bankrupt,' Hazel pointed out. 'Especially if you're bankrupt. You know, I've sort of fallen for her, too. Why not give her to someone who can pay?'

'Maybe I could call her Bunji.' Kiara sounded thoughtful. 'It means a mate. A friend.'

Hazel nodded. It had to be an indigenous

word. Kiara's gorgeous colouring—along with her own name—was due to her grandmother being indigenous so she knew a lot more about the language than Hazel did.

But Kiara was looking doubtful now. 'Who am I kidding? How could I give such a dog to a ten-year-old?'

'Give her to the uncle. He sounds like he needs a friend, as much if not more than his niece. And hey, if he falls for Bunji, he might even be prepared to backpay for her treatment. How's that for a thought?'

'They really don't want a dog. Besides, I'd have to stay there. A week at least, he stipulated, and who's going to take care of this place? I can't ask you to take more time off. I can't afford to pay anyone. The whole thing's impossible.'

Hazel frowned, trying to think up a solution. And then her phone beeped and almost immediately beeped again.

'Two messages? I'd better see what that's about,' she said, stripping off her gloves. 'I'm worried about Ben.'

The first text wasn't a message about Ben this time, either. It was another text from Finn and this one made Hazel catch her breath.

I'm sorry. You're right. About everything. This *is* real and I can't do it by myself.

Oh… *Finn*… The emotional exhaustion of today's events was making it too hard to protect herself by not getting too close. And then she opened the message that had come in straight after and staying angry with him or even deeply disappointed suddenly became a lot harder.

I really need you, Hazel.

'I need to go,' she told Kiara.

'Ben?'

'I…no. I'm sure he's okay but I would like to see for myself. And you'll want the results on those blood samples as soon as possible.' Hazel was going to arrange to have the samples analysed at work.

Kiara nodded. 'No worries. We've done all we can for the moment. I'll finish up and get her settled. Thanks so much for your help.'

'Think about what I said before. About giving Bunji to that uncle. Maybe it's true that people—and dogs—come into our lives for a reason.'

And babies?

Hazel sent a message back to Finn as she went out to her van.

Out at Two Tails but on my way back. See you soon.

CHAPTER FOUR

WAITING FOR MORE than an hour for Hazel to get back and then across the city was winding the knot of tension in Finn's gut so tight the pain was becoming intense but, in comparison to everything else exploding in his life right now, it was insignificant.

When Hazel didn't pick up when he called her, Finn's heart sank to new levels, but she called back within a minute or two.

'I had to pull over,' she said. 'A nineteen-seventies Morris Minor doesn't run to Bluetooth.'

'When you get to my apartment block, park around the back by the rubbish bins. There's a fire escape door and you can get in with a code. I'll text it to you. You'll have to come up the stairs rather than take the lift.' His huff of laughter was ironic. 'Sorry about that. Who would have thought that living in a penthouse would have its disadvantages?'

'What's with all the cloak and dagger stuff?'

'Someone leaked at least part of this story to the media. Probably that cameraman who thought the whole drama was so amusing. They might not know everything but they know that something's going on and they've set up camp in front of the building. They caught Shannon when she was arriving but, luckily, she could tell the truth when she told them she had no idea what they were talking about.'

'Shannon's there?' There was an odd note in Hazel's voice. Was she about to change her mind about coming because he had someone with him?

'Not for long,' he told her grimly. 'Apparently she doesn't "do" babies.'

There was a heartbeat's silence on the other end of the line. He thought he could hear Hazel take in a quick breath. 'So you've taken Ellie home? How *is* she?'

Finn walked across the vast living area of his penthouse apartment. To one side, he could see Shannon on the balcony, with its stunning, panoramic view of the Coogee coastline. She was currently pouting at the phone in her hand, probably adjusting its position to capture the lights of the cityscape behind her. The sliding doors were firmly shut to keep the smoke from her cigarette outside. Finn spared her no more than a weary glance. Ahead of him, tucked up inside a nest of cushions on the couch, was the baby. It felt like she hadn't stopped crying since he'd brought her home after the visit from the police and a representative for Social Services. He knew that Hazel would be able to hear the sound of the miserable infant clearly now.

'Oh…' The sympathetic sound in his ear gave Finn a very odd sensation—surely it couldn't be tears forming? He hadn't cried since…well, since Ellie. The first Ellie, that was. There was a note in that low sound that gave him hope that Hazel wasn't mad at him any more, even if she did think he was a complete failure as a human being. That she might understand that it wasn't just the baby who was feeling unbearably miserable. That he could possibly depend on her to be on his side and, in this moment, it was the best feeling he could hope for.

'I need to pick her up,' was all he said. 'She might be hungry again. I'll text you that code in a minute.'

Shannon came inside as he was juggling the baby in the crook of one arm and read-

ing the instructions on the back of the can
of milk formula. She stood there, looking
impossibly gorgeous in her skin-tight, se-
quinned black evening dress with a thigh
high split and deep neckline that left virtu-
ally nothing to the imagination.

Looking…fake?

Looking absolutely furious, that was for
sure.

'I can't believe you're doing this to me,
Finn. You knew how important it was to be
seen at this fundraiser this evening. There
are potential sponsors for me there that could
make or break my career.'

'I've said I'm sorry. I didn't exactly plan
for this to happen.' Finn carefully measured
a scoop of the creamy powder into the bottle
that already contained cooled boiled water.
When did being so popular on social media
become a 'career' exactly? When the number of people who followed you got past half
a million? Would there be a degree in social
media at university one of these years, to
give it the status of a *real* career?

'If we hurried, we could still get there in
time. Surely you know someone who could
look after it for a while? Or take it away?'

It? Even if he hadn't exactly dismissed the
baby as no more than an unwanted object

himself, he'd acted as if it was, hadn't he? A problem to get sorted. Something to hide so that nobody else found out. He looked down at the small bundle he was holding. She was still crying, but it was a whimper rather than a howl and that felt like a win. He screwed the top onto the bottle and shook it to dissolve the formula.

He could see why anybody would think his girlfriend's lifestyle was fake but *he* had a real career as a very successful veterinary surgeon. Just because he'd added an extra dimension to that career by becoming unexpectedly well known on television didn't mean he was fake. And why did it matter so much what Hazel thought, anyway?

Because, deep down, he was ashamed of how he'd felt when he'd considered the possibility that he was this baby's grandfather? He'd seen a reflection of himself in Shannon's reaction.

A grandfather? As in a whole generation removed? Do you know how old that makes you look? How utterly un*sexy that is?*

Oh, yeah…he knew. But maybe he was getting used to it. Like the way he was getting over the shock of the weight and warmth of holding his baby in his arms after Hazel had shoved Ellie into them, hours and hours ago now. He would have thought that it wouldn't be much different from holding a big puppy, like a fluffy Old English sheepdog, perhaps, but, oddly, nothing in his career had really prepared him for how this felt.

It was more than simply holding a child this young. It was the idea that he might have a connection with another person that came with expectations. Responsibilities. The potential for heartache...

Things that he wasn't anywhere near ready to even think of including in his life. He was a bachelor and that suited him perfectly. A bachelor with a successful career, the kind of wealth that meant he was safe from ever having to worry about not being able to pay his bills and...okay...it wasn't exactly unpleasant to be so popular with women.

'Why don't you go alone?' he said to Shannon. 'You can go out the fire escape and you won't need to talk to anybody.'

'Why should I have to sneak around? *I* haven't done anything wrong.'

'It might save you a bit of temporary embarrassment.'

'What will embarrass me is to attend a function without my boyfriend. A function that he was the one who was invited to. We're supposed to be a couple. How can I go on my own?'

'You'd be fine. You don't need to be on my arm to attract attention, you know.'

'Don't flatter yourself,' Shannon snapped. 'When we're out in public, it's my arm *you're* on, not the other way round. How many followers do *you* have?'

The chime of his doorbell suggested that he had at least one and Finn was only too happy to check the camera and see that it was Hazel. He had to step back not only to allow Hazel to enter his apartment but for Shannon to have room to leave because that was what she appeared to be doing as she marched into the foyer with her clutch purse under her arm. She paused when she noticed Hazel, however.

'You work with Finn, don't you? Have you come to babysit, then?' She was glancing at her watch as she spoke. Working out if there was still enough time for Finn to get changed into a tuxedo and make an appearance at the fundraiser? As her man bag?

'No.' It was Finn who answered before Hazel could even blink. 'Of course she hasn't. Hazel's here to help me for a bit, that's all.'

Shannon flicked that extraordinary mane of blonde hair that brushed her buttocks as she looked over her shoulder at Finn.

'Call me.' The ice in her voice was not a warm invitation. 'When you've got rid of it.'

The look she gave the baby in Finn's arms was a death glare. And maybe, a few hours ago, Finn might have been relieved if he could have walked away from this problem with no more than a look of such extreme distaste but Shannon's attitude was suddenly making him feel…what, protective?

He was feeling something, anyway. The numbness of feeling like a stunned mullet with this serve that life had thrown at him from left field was wearing off. Finn suspected that the death glare had been successful, though. Not that it was the baby who would suffer, he'd make sure of that, but it definitely felt as if his relationship with Shannon might well have just had a death blow delivered.

Not that he had the slightest inclination to waste any more emotional energy on the woman who had, if truth were told, been an annoyingly high-maintenance girlfriend.

Fake, a small voice whispered in the back of his head. *Like you...*

Oh, dear…

The fury Shannon Summers left in her wake was palpable. Had Hazel caught the finale of a much bigger row? Maybe that was why Finn looked so incredibly wrecked. His collar was unbuttoned and his sleeves loosely rolled up. He had a five o'clock shadow that was almost designer stubble and his hair was standing on end, as if he'd combed it with his fingers many times.

And, heaven help her, but he'd never looked more attractive. On any level that Hazel could think of and both her body and heart were automatically responding. She wanted to smooth his ruffled hair. Offer him comfort and reassurance that everything was going to be okay. And, yeah...there was a ridiculously strong desire to drift close enough to try and find out whether kissing him would make the world and its problems vanish, at least for a little while.

The desire was not only ridiculous because Finn's girlfriend had only just walked out of the door and she knew how horrified Finn would be if she hit on him, it was totally inappropriate given that the man was holding a whimpering infant on one arm as he led Hazel into the living area of his apartment, trying unsuccessfully to get Ellie to accept the bottle of milk at the same time.

'It might work better if you sit down,' Hazel suggested.

To his credit, Finn didn't ask her to take the baby. He did sit down and he tried again, by slotting the teat into a tiny mouth that was wide open in mid-howl. Some milk dribbled in but got spluttered out and the intensity of the howling increased. Hazel managed to resist the urge to step in and help—until Finn looked up and she could swear she saw tears in his eyes.

'I'm hopeless at this,' he said.

Hazel was quite sure she could actually *feel* her heart melting as a liquid warmth spread through her body. Nothing on earth could have stopped her trying to help. Trying to do whatever it took to make Finn at least a little happier.

She sat on the sofa beside him and took the baby into her own arms. For a moment, she just held the infant against her heart and jiggled her, bending her head to murmur a bit of soothing baby talk and finally planting a kiss on those astonishingly soft curls. She touched Ellie's cheek with the teat of the bottle and then, as the baby opened her mouth and turned her head sideways, it felt as if it was her choice to accept the milk and it wasn't being forced on her.

The moment that the howling changed to

sucking noises, Finn dropped his head back against the couch and let out a loud sigh.

'Thank you,' was all he said.

They sat there in silence for a minute. And then another. And it seemed as if an out-of-control world was also pausing to let out a bit of a sigh. Hazel was sinking into the feeling of holding this baby in her arms. She was also very aware that Finn was sitting right beside her. She could almost feel the warmth of his thigh so close to her own. If she moved, just a fraction, they would be touching...

Hastily, she broke the silence to shut down that thought. 'So...tell me what's been happening. I gather Shannon's not very impressed with developments?'

Finn's hand gesture dismissed his beautiful girlfriend as totally irrelevant and Hazel couldn't help a frisson of relief. He deserved a real relationship—with a real person—not something that was as staged as food photography for a recipe book.

'I talked to the police. And someone from Social Services. We agreed that the important thing was to keep the baby safe and that, if there is a family connection, the mother might be more likely to approach me than official channels and also that it could be easier to put Elena into foster care than take her out again immediately so they were prepared to let me look after her.'

'Wow...' Hazel was impressed that Finn had even considered it as an option. 'That was brave.'

Finn had covered his eyes with his hand and was rubbing his temples with his thumb and middle finger. 'It's only for a day or two. Maybe three. I also got hold of the guy who knows about the DNA testing and he came and took swabs from me and Elena. I've paid a considerable amount for an urgent service, which can be through in forty-eight to seventy-two hours if I'm lucky. It might be a lot less time than that if whoever left the baby comes back for her.'

Hazel's gaze drifted to the bags on his kitchen counter in this open plan living area. 'I know I was out of town for a good few hours, but how on earth did you manage to fit shopping in? You've even got a car seat there. Did Anna help?'

'No. It was the woman from Social Services—Margaret. She's been really helpful. Anna did call, though. She wanted me to know that your spaniel is doing really well. He woke up, had a drink of water and even wagged his tail. She topped up his analgesia and he should sleep through the rest of the night now. There's no need for you to go in.'

'Okay… I guess I can stay here and help you, then.'

When Finn shook his head, it felt like a rejection. But then he took a deep breath. 'I can't stay here,' he told her. 'Not with the media camped outside. The mother of this baby—or possibly the father, as you suggested—would be just as unlikely to go near them as turn up at a police station. They could well be scared of getting into trouble. I'm not about to give any press statements, either—not until I know what I'm actually dealing with and I won't know that until the DNA results come through.'

'What will you do when you know?'

'If Elena's no relation to me, we'll go public and try and find her mother.'

'And if she is?'

Finn met her gaze with a direct look that was unlike any Hazel had ever seen before. It looked, oddly, as if he'd just grown up a whole lot more.

'If she is my grandchild, then I'll step up and do the right thing.'

Oh… Hazel couldn't tell him how proud she was of this new attitude. There was relief to be found as well because she hadn't been that blinded by how she felt about Finn. He *was* a good person, beneath the celebrity exterior. Someone it wasn't stupid to be more than a bit in love with.

'That's where you come in,' Finn said.

She couldn't meet his gaze in case he saw even a flash of what had just gone through her head. 'Oh…?'

'I'm going to go out to my weekend place. The house I've got up in the Blue Mountains and I'll lie low there with the baby until we know which direction this is going to go in. I'm hoping we can sneak out the back and use your van and that way we'll escape any attention from the paparazzi camped out the front.'

Hazel had heard about the property Finn had purchased some time ago. There'd been pictures of it in a magazine article and she knew it was only a little further into the mountainous region than Two Tails. It was quite a long way to go to offer what would be a taxi service for a man and a baby, mind you, but Hazel found herself nodding slowly. This was a way she could offer some real help—to someone she cared about far more than was probably wise.

'I'm also hoping that you'll stay there with me,' Finn added. 'At least for just one night?'

Just one night…

It sounded like the title of a romantic movie or a book.

Just One Night
A fantasy starring James Finlay from *Call the Vet*
Also starring newcomer Hazel David-son
Oh…and a cute baby

'I know you've just done that round trip but I can drive out there.' Finn sounded hope-ful. 'And it would be much more sensible to stay the night than driving back again, wouldn't it? I gave my housekeeper a call a while back and she's made sure there are beds made up and food in the fridge.'

Hazel found herself smiling wryly. She'd already known better than to buy into any fantasy but that tiny moment in time had been rather delicious. Finn interpreted her smile rather differently.

'You'll do it?' There was more than hope in Finn's tone now. It sounded almost like excitement. 'Oh, man… I can't tell you how grateful I am.' Finn leaned sideways and planted a kiss on her cheek. 'I love you, Hazel. You're the best friend anyone could have.'

The friend zone. It was better than no zone at all, wasn't it? It was a bit of a warning bell that a platonic kiss on the cheek could send spirals of sensation all the way to the tips of Hazel's toes but how could she possibly let Finn down? He needed her and she couldn't deny that it felt good. Something had changed between them since this drama had begun unfolding. Hazel had felt like he was seeing her properly for the first time. She was also seeing something new in Finn. A maturity that she hadn't noticed before. And that moment when she'd seen what looked like tears in his eyes as he admitted how out of his depth he was? Well…that kind of felt like a glimpse of the man behind the image that James Finlay presented to the world. Possibly to himself as well?

Whatever. Something was changing. Something important.

Hazel was holding a now soundly sleeping baby. She got to her feet and put Ellie carefully back into a nest that had been made with cushions at one end of the sofa and tucked the fuzzy duck blanket around her.

Then she straightened her back and smiled at Finn. Properly, this time.

'Let's get this show on the road, then, shall we?'

CHAPTER FIVE

IN THE FIRST soft light of dawn, Hazel opened the French doors in the bedroom she'd used in James Finlay's country house and stepped out…into a fairy tale. Well, she'd actually stepped out onto a veranda, but it was a super-sized version of the one she loved at Kiara's cottage and the difference wasn't just in how enormous it was. Or the generous scattering of gorgeous wicker couches and chairs with soft cushions that were begging to have someone curl up in them and chill. They were just part of a much bigger picture. Another dimension, almost.

The wrought iron lace on the outside edge of the roof provided an anchor for a wisteria vine that must have been growing for decades to have become so luxuriant. White racemes of fragrant flowers that had to measure half a metre created a curtain through which Hazel could catch glimpses of neatly clipped box hedges in a formal rose garden, a pond, fenced paddocks that looked like lawns and tall, tall gum trees that marked the edge of untouched bushland.

The scent of the flowers was intoxicating. So was the sound of birdsong including the laughter of a kookaburra, as the Blue Mountain wildlife woke up, until it was drowned out by the screech of cockatoos. Hazel couldn't see the yellow crest on their heads, but the flash of white wings was spectacular and she followed their flight until they settled on the branches of one of the massive gum trees, making it look like large, pale flowers had suddenly bloomed.

'Sleep well?'

Hazel jumped, her head turning swiftly to the figure who'd walked around the next corner of a veranda that could well be wrapped right around this enormous, colonial house. She hadn't taken much in by the time she and Finn had finally arrived here at nearly two a.m. after their dramatic, secret escape from his apartment that had been like being photoshopped into a spy movie.

'I went out like a light,' she confessed. 'I'm sorry I didn't help you get Ellie to bed.'

'Bed? What's that?' Finn's smile was crooked and he looked even more rumpled and unkempt than he had when Hazel had seen him yesterday evening after responding to his plea for help. 'I did put her in the cot. I even started to get ready for bed myself but…it didn't quite work out.'

'Mmm…' Hazel was taking in the rest of Finn's appearance now. He had bare feet beneath his jeans and a shirt that was completely unbuttoned. The only part of his chest that wasn't revealed was the bit that was covered by a bundle of blanket wrapped baby lying on one arm. A baby that was making hiccupping sounds, which could either be the end or beginning of a much louder session of misery.

The shadow of beard on Finn's face was even darker in this early light and there were deep lines at the corners of his eyes, as if it was hard work to be keeping them open. Hazel felt guilty that she'd had a few hours of deep sleep in the most comfortable bed ever. She also felt a rather powerful blend of pity and pride for Finn, who was facing up to what had to be an overwhelming challenge—one that he could have easily sidestepped by handing Ellie over to Social Services and an experienced, emergency foster family.

'Let me take her,' she offered, reaching

out for the baby. 'You might feel better after a shower?'

'She might kick off again if I move her and this is the quietest she's been in more than an hour. Coffee is what I need. If you could bring me a large mug—black, no sugar—I would be eternally in your debt. Oh…and Beanie here will be needing another bottle, I expect.'

'Beanie?'

'It's that hair. It looks like a hat. Have you ever seen a baby with so much hair?'

'She could give a labradoodle puppy a run for its money in the cute stakes, that's for sure.' Hazel resisted the urge to touch the baby, who was still making squeaking noises. 'Coffee it is. I'll be back in no time.'

Hazel was smiling but she was also backing away, relieved to have a mission that meant she could duck into her bedroom on the way. How had she not registered that she was wearing her pyjamas? Soft, silky harem style pants and a clingy singlet top that did nothing to disguise her top half. It had, in fact, not done enough to actually cover her top half with that gap of a couple of inches between its hem and the elastic of the pants. She hadn't brushed her hair, either, so she had a tangle of mousy frizz brushing her

bare shoulders and it hadn't occurred to her
to even splash water on her face before greeting the day, let alone try and improve her
appearance with a kiss of any makeup.

It all added up to the horrific thought that
she might as well have been naked. Not that
Finn had seemed taken aback in any way,
fortunately, but he was too shell-shocked
and exhausted to notice and, besides, he'd
never seen her as potentially physically attractive anyway, had he? Hazel threw on the
same clothes she'd been wearing since she'd
changed out of her scrubs yesterday, dragged
a comb through her hair and was securing it
into a messy bun as she went off to look for
the kitchen she vaguely remembered Finn
pointing out when they'd arrived here in the
early hours of this morning.

'Make yourself at home,' he'd said. 'What's
mine is yours.'

And wouldn't that be a dream come true?
Hazel thought. Her bedsit apartment could
have slotted into any one of these wide
hallways with their high ceilings, let alone
the huge rooms leading off them. Polished
wooden floors had beautiful rugs and there
were so many windows there was already
enough light to know that the house would
be flooded with sunshine later in the day.

The kitchen had a flagged, stone floor and a French country theme that could have—and probably had—been photographed for some 'home and living' magazine.

A huge, double-door fridge was well stocked with food and a walk-in pantry looked like a miniature supermarket. Hazel had no clue how to drive what looked like a commercial coffee maker, but she found a plunger jug and a tin of what smelled like freshly roasted and ground beans. She put some wholegrain bread in a toaster and then tackled a mess on the bench that was a clear sign that Finn had been making up baby formula under stress in the last few hours. She had no idea what he might like on his toast, so she went with what had long been comfort food for herself.

The way Finn's face lit up when he saw the plate piled with toast and its covering of melted butter and a generous amount of crunchy peanut butter gave Hazel a surprising jolt of pleasure. She put the tray down on a table beside the chair he was sitting on.

'I thought you might need some sustenance.'

Finn was carefully lifting a mug of coffee, keeping it well away from the baby. He closed his eyes as he took a sip and then another. When he opened them, he was looking directly at Hazel, his gaze so warm, she could feel the heat.

'Perfect,' he murmured. 'Thank you.'

'You're welcome.' Hazel picked up her own mug and shifted her gaze before she could start reading something that wasn't there in the warmth of that look. 'Oh... Are those kangaroos in that paddock?'

Finn spoke around a mouthful of toast. 'Yep. I often see them at this time of day.' He swallowed his mouthful. 'Not often enough, to be honest. Every time I do get out here I wonder why I don't do it every weekend. Or live out here and commute. I love this place.'

'It's gorgeous,' Hazel agreed. She helped herself to a piece of the toast. 'What do you use the paddocks for? Do you have horses?'

Finn shook his head. 'I have a couple who manage the place for me who have a farm nearby. Sandra does the housework and shopping and so on. Her husband looks after the grounds. He mows the paddocks with his tractor to keep them tidy.' His eyes drifted shut, not to savour the taste of anything this time—it looked as if he simply couldn't keep them open any longer.

'Why don't you go and get a few hours' sleep?' Hazel suggested. 'I'm not rostered on for the morning clinic and I'm only in Theatre for a few routine desexing surgeries early this afternoon so I can look after Ellie for a bit. Give her some breakfast and a bath, perhaps. I guess you'll be wanting to come in with me in the van to pick up your car?'

But Finn shook his head. 'I don't want to go near my apartment building. I really don't want this getting splashed all over the media. Which means I'll probably have to stay away from work, too, even if it's where Beanie's mother might go to make contact. I'll give Nigel and Anna a call later and sort out cover.' He was watching Hazel as he spoke. 'I could organise cover for you, too…'

She raised an eyebrow. 'Why? I'll be back in the city in plenty of time to go home and get changed and still be early enough for any pre-operative checks before surgery.'

Finn was holding her gaze over the sleeping baby. 'I thought I might be able to persuade you to hang around for a day or two.'

'What for?' Hazel mentally stomped on an errant flash of hope that Finn genuinely wanted more time with her simply because he liked being with her by deliberately frowning. 'Oh, I get it. You want me to look after Ellie for you. You need a babysitter?' She broke the eye contact, reaching for a piece of toast even though eating something was the last thing she really wanted to do. 'Reality's a bit of a shocker, isn't it?'

The reminder of yesterday's accusation that he was fake wasn't fair.

Thanks to how exhausted he currently was, it was actually rather hurtful. He was doing his best here and he'd made a point of not disturbing Hazel's sleep in the last few hours as he tried, and failed, to get the baby to settle.

He just wanted her company. Was that so weird? He wanted to be with someone who could share the trauma of the current crisis in his life. Someone he felt comfortable enough to be around when he looked like hell and was only half dressed. When they were in their pyjamas and there wasn't even a hint of any underlying sexual agenda—although, to be completely honest, it had been a rather pleasant surprise to see more of Hazel than he ever had before. More importantly, she was someone who somehow knew that peanut butter toast was his favourite guilty pleasure. And Hazel had never been overly impressed with his fame or fortune, either. He knew she didn't follow him on any social media platform and she certainly had no connection to any of the groups he mixed with in his fast-moving, A-list social life.

And the clincher? He now realised that Hazel could see right through him despite his oh, so carefully constructed persona. She was quite probably the only person who could recognise what was still there deep inside and, while it was just as much of a shock as having a baby land on his doorstep, a part of Finn couldn't deny that it might be a good thing that someone had the guts to call him out on how he was living his life. Did he *want* someone to see him for who he really was? Or had been, anyway?

No. That part of his life had been left behind long ago.

Until now, anyway. Until a baby named after the girl who'd pretty much saved his life turned up. Finn shook his head to dismiss that flash of thought and the action prompted him to speak with absolute sincerity.

'No way. I would never ask you to babysit. I'm taking total responsibility for Beanie. It's just that… I don't know, it's going to be a lonely couple of days out here by myself and… I kind of like the idea of spending some time with you. Away from work. We've never really done that, have we?'

Her gaze grazed his. Just long enough

for him to register the same feeling he'd got when she'd reacted to his suggestion that she hung around for a day or two. He hadn't been able to interpret her expression but whatever it was, it had morphed into suspicion with that frown. This time, she looked away before he had any hope of gauging her reaction but it might not have made any difference, he decided. Women were experts in hiding what was going on in their heads, weren't they?

'I just thought you might like a change of scene. How long is it since you had a few days off?'

'A while,' Hazel admitted.

'What did you do with them?' Finn was genuinely interested. 'Where did you go?'

Hazel smiled. 'Not far. I was helping Kiara build some new pens out at the refuge.'

Ah…the refuge. Hazel's passion. Finn was having a lightbulb moment and it centred around the dog she'd named after a treasured pet in her childhood.

'You know how you said you'd rescue Ben if you didn't live in a bedsit?'

Hazel really looked startled by this turn in the conversation. Wary, even. 'Yeah? So…?'

'Bring him here,' Finn suggested. 'You could look after him here until he's sorted.'

Hazel was staring at him as if he was

talking nonsense. 'Ben's hardly going to be sorted in a couple of days. I'll have to take him to Two Tails even if it's not ideal. Kiara has way more than she needs to deal with at the moment.' Her sigh was heartfelt. 'And I'm responsible for a rather big part of that after what happened yesterday.'

'What happened?' Finn could feel himself frowning. How could Kiara have been affected by the dramatic events that had unfolded in his own life yesterday?

'I was on my way to see her after...' Hazel looked away. 'After I left work.'

That hesitation was telling. What she meant was, after she'd walked out having discovered how disappointing a person Finn was.

'I found an abandoned dog on the side of the road. A really horribly abused dog. I took it to Two Tails because there wasn't anything else I *could* do and now Kiara has got a dog on her hands that's going to take all the time and energy she's got and all the money she *hasn't* got for weeks and weeks.'

'So it would be a lot better if you could look after Ben.'

Hazel shrugged. 'As I said, a couple of days wouldn't make much of a difference.'

'You *could* stay here for as long as you

like,' Ben said. 'I hardly ever get the chance to come out here and it's a shame that a place this beautiful doesn't get used.' This was the first time Finn was feeling guilty about it, however. Was that because he could suddenly see it as Hazel might see it? As an advertisement of wealth and privilege that was no more than a staged background for part of a perfect life?

Hazel wasn't saying anything. She was staring straight ahead of her even though there was nothing much to see through the dangly flowers other than his empty paddocks.

'So…you'd let me live here with Ben until he was well enough to rehome? In return for keeping you company and helping out with Ellie?'

Finn nodded.

'We could cover each other if there was something urgent to do in the city. You could do your surgery this afternoon and then come back out, with Ben. And whatever else you need to get settled here. I could go in if…if there was something important to do.' He caught the look Hazel gave him. 'I'm not talking about media stuff. I meant talking to the police or a solicitor or something. I still have no idea what I'm going to do if those DNA results come back positive.'

'Mmm.'

There was a thoughtful silence that hung in the air between them. Hazel looked away and then back to hold his gaze. 'Those empty paddocks…' she murmured. 'In particular, that one with the stable block…'

Finn blinked. 'Yes…?'

'You remember that donkey I told you about? The one with the feet that are so bad it can't walk? Could it come too—if another place hasn't been found yet? For as long as I'm here with Ben?'

She was clearly bargaining but Finn was prepared to do whatever it took, within reason, to persuade her to stay. It wasn't as if she was asking for something for herself— she was obviously going to base her decision on how many other creatures she could help. How many people would do that?

Nobody could accuse Hazel Davidson of being fake. What you saw was what you got. A warm, compassionate, genuine human being who was also intelligent and a highly skilled professional. It felt like something was melting a little, deep inside Finn's chest. She was special, that was what Hazel was. Funny, but he'd never noticed before that her eyes matched her name. A golden, hazel brown with shiny flecks in them that matched the glints in her hair the sun was just beginning to catch as it rose high enough to see over the gum trees. She had a cute nose, as well, come to think of it, and lips that looked…really soft. Kissable, even…? Good grief…that startling thought needed to be pushed away as fast as possible.

'I think that can be arranged,' he heard himself say, relieved at how calm he sounded, given what he'd just been thinking about. 'When I've had a shower, I'll ring Sandra. They keep horses and I know they've got a float. I could probably arrange for them to go and collect the donkey. They'll know a good, local farrier, too, who could start treating its feet.'

The bundle in his arms was starting to feel very damp. It was also starting to squirm and he could see a small face getting rather red as the energy was gathered to communicate the need for a clean nappy. Or breakfast. Or maybe just a change of carer. It felt like pressure, anyway, and it was enough to trigger an alarm bell—maybe one that had already started ringing when he'd had the astonishing notion of Hazel Davidson being kissable.

'As long as I don't end up having to look

after them,' he added as a warning. 'I have a rule about dependants. Like pets or kids or wives. I don't do them. Not on a long-term basis. Not on any basis, really...'

And yet here he was, with a baby in his arms and hoping, rather a lot, that he was about to get a woman as a companion twenty-four-seven for the immediate future, along with an injured dog and a lame donkey. Was he out of his mind?

But Hazel was smiling at him and, for some reason, Finn was feeling a lot better than he might have expected.

'Wives? Plural?' Her smile widened. 'I'm learning quite a lot about you, Dr Finn.'

'So you're going to stick around?' He thought that smile was already giving him the answer he wanted but he needed reassurance. 'You might learn even more of my secrets.'

'How could I resist?' Hazel stood up and came to take the baby from his arms. 'Now, go and have that shower. And take a nap. We'll sort everything out if the offer's still there when you're not totally sleep deprived.'

Finn smiled back at her.

He wasn't going to change his mind. Having Hazel around to share the roller coaster he had a feeling this crisis could well become was nothing short of a lifeline.

When Hazel took the small, heart-shaped silver frame from her bedside table and put it with the items she considered essential for at least the next week or so, it felt as if she were leaving her bedsit apartment behind for ever because she was taking her most precious possession with her—the photo of her first dog called Ben.

When she gently settled her second dog called Ben into the back of her van and began the return journey to Finn's beautiful property in the Blue Mountains, it felt like...

Oh, help...it felt as if she were going home.

She wasn't. She needed to remember that this was temporary. She might be going to be living a fantasy for as long as it took Ben to recover from his surgery and for his broken bones to heal but she'd better not get too used to it. At some point, she would have to find a new home for Ben and return to her bedsit and her fulltime job at Coogee Beach Animal Hospital. She would also need to find a new home for that donkey, as well. What on earth had she been thinking making a new rescue animal part of the deal?

Finn had run a staff meeting via video link

when Hazel had gone in to work at lunchtime. The staff all knew about yesterday's drama of the baby being abandoned and Finn's popularity was evident in their willingness to do whatever they could to help. Everybody was put on alert for any potential contact from anyone associated with the baby, with instructions to be non-judgmental and quick to offer any assistance asked for. Both Hazel's and Finn's workloads were picked up by others until further notice, with plans to review strategies once the results of the DNA tests made the situation clearer.

'It just goes to show,' Hazel said when she phoned Kiara on her way out of the city, 'that it wouldn't be that hard for me to get some time off for personal reasons. Not immediately, maybe, what with this baby crisis, but sometime soon—so if you change your mind about taking that job offer with the uncle I'd be able to look after Two Tails.'

'I won't be changing my mind,' Kiara said. 'I don't even like the guy and I don't have a suitable dog, anyway. Bunji's not going to be fit to rehome for a very long time. If ever.'

'How is she today?'

'It's still touch and go. I can't even think about anything else.'

'Did someone call you to get the details about that donkey?'

'Yes.' She could hear a wry smile in Kiara's tone. 'How on earth did you persuade Finn to let you do that?'

'I thought Ben and I would need some company. We could be there for quite a while. He'll have to have his activity restricted for the next eight to ten weeks. I imagine the baby business will be sorted within the next few days and then Finn will be back in his penthouse at the beach. You should see his house, Kiara. It's one of those amazing colonial mansions. Actually, you *could* see his house. It's not that far from Birralong. Fifteen minutes' drive at the most.'

'I'm not going anywhere if I can help it. Not until I know that Bunji's going to make it. How's Ben doing?'

'I'm happy with how it's going. He's still groggy after the anaesthetic and we had to carry him outside to toilet but…he's a lovely old boy. I think he recognised me when I went in to collect him. Or maybe he just loves everybody.'

'I doubt that, after the way he's been treated. He must trust you. Hey, I need to go and look after Bunji. Good luck with getting Ben settled. Call me if I can help.'

* * *

Finn was only too happy to help Hazel get Ben settled in. He helped her unbandage the dog's leg to check his surgical wound and then redress it, offered the leftover poached chicken from his lunch for Ben's first meal, carried the little dog outside himself to do his business and then found a way to barricade the door to a laundry area to give the dog a safe, confined space to sleep.

It felt good to be able to help with Ben. It put them on a more even footing and he didn't feel guilty about asking for Hazel's help with the baby because that help went on for many hours before the baby was finally asleep in the bassinette that Finn had had delivered today, along with many other items from a Sydney baby shop. It felt good to be making toasted sandwiches and choosing one of the better wines from his extensive cellar to have a very late dinner ready for Hazel after she'd unpacked the last of the things she'd brought from her apartment to make her stay here more comfortable.

Oddly, though, Hazel didn't look too happy at the offering he'd arranged on one of the wrought iron tables on the veranda. He'd even remembered to turn on the fairy lights that were wound through the wisteria vine on the fretwork and, even if he did say so himself, he thought he'd set up an irresistibly attractive corner. A scene with the kind of romance that most women loved.

'You don't drink red wine? I can find something white? Or champagne? Or don't you like cheese toasties?'

Hazel laughed. 'Are you kidding? Who doesn't love cheese toasties? I was just surprised, that's all.'

'Okay…' Finn picked up a glass of wine and sat down. 'I get it. Sorry—I'm just not much of a cook and Ben ate the last of the chicken Sandra made for my lunch.'

'Oh, I didn't mean I expected you to cook.' Hazel put the baby monitor down on the table and picked up one of the sandwiches, a handful of serviettes and the other glass of wine. She gave Finn an apologetic glance as she sank down onto the feather-stuffed cushions on the other end of the couch. 'I was just surprised because bread was totally forbidden the last time a man made my dinner and… oh, wow…this is *so* crispy. Did you fry these rather than toast them?'

'Yes. There's bacon in there as well.' But Finn was frowning. 'You're not gluten intolerant or something, are you?'

'Not at all. It was just the latest diet I was

supposed to be on. Wasn't my idea.' Hazel smiled at Finn and then took a bite of the sandwich. 'Mmm…this is delicious.'

Finn said nothing but he was thinking fast. Who on earth would have been trying to force Hazel to follow a diet she didn't want? More than one diet, even, if going without bread was part of the 'latest' one. A boyfriend, perhaps? Come to think of it, he'd met Hazel's partner a long time ago, at some work function and…he hadn't liked him much at all.

'What was his name?' he said aloud. 'That tall, skinny guy you were living with when you first came to work with me?'

'Michael.' Hazel reached for her wine glass. 'But I didn't say it was him that wouldn't let me eat bread, did I?'

'*Was* it?'

Hazel shrugged, not meeting his gaze. 'He's long gone. It really doesn't matter now.'

But Finn had the feeling that it did. He was suddenly glad that he hadn't made her a plate of salad for dinner. He was also feeling mortified on Hazel's behalf that someone she had been in a relationship with had been trying to change her in such a blatant manner. How could it not make you feel like you weren't good enough the way you were?

He didn't know Hazel well enough to try and offer some kind of reassurance, though, so he simply smiled as she took another bite of her sandwich.

'Good?'

'Mmm.'

They sat there in companionable silence after that, until Hazel had eaten all she wanted and was stifling a huge yawn.

'Go to bed,' Finn said. 'I'll take the monitor and get up if Beanie starts crying.'

Hazel shook her head. 'I'm happy to get up. That way, I can check on Ben, too.'

They both stood up at the same time. They both reached for the monitor handset at the same time. They both pulled away as their hands touched but then they both smiled at each other.

'You can have it tonight,' Finn conceded. 'I'll have it tomorrow night. After that, we might not need to fight over it.'

Weird that it felt like getting this crisis sorted and baby Elena back to where she belonged might happen too soon. He felt like he was just getting to know Hazel a lot better. And he liked it. He liked it a lot.

Finn's smile faded. He was standing very close to Hazel and she was still smiling at him. Without thinking he reached up and touched her cheek with the back of his fore-finger.

'It's a good thing that Michael is long gone,' he said. 'The guy was a complete jerk.'

There was something in Hazel's gaze that he'd never seen before despite it looking like something that could have been there for ever. Something…lost? It made him want to take her into his arms and hug her. Instead, he just held her gaze.

'Don't let anyone think you're not beautiful just the way you are,' he added softly. 'Because it's not true.'

It felt like time had stopped. Or maybe Hazel had just frozen, shocked by what he was saying. She didn't believe him, did she? But what else could he say that might convince her?

Maybe he didn't need to say anything. The idea of showing her was a lightbulb moment, like tempting her to stay here by offering a place for Ben to recuperate. Only this flash of inspiration wasn't purely intellectual. It was more of a physical thing.

Because…because Hazel really was beautiful and…and he really did want to kiss her.

Just gently. Good grief, he wasn't trying to seduce her or anything. He just wanted her to know that he meant what he'd said. And that she deserved something a hell of a lot better than someone who didn't think she was perfect just the way she was.

And…maybe it was his imagination but it looked as though Hazel *wanted* him to kiss her. She certainly wasn't ducking for cover as his mouth drifted slowly closer to her own. And then his lips brushed hers and it was Finn who felt like he needed to duck for cover because there was a strange sensation that came with that barely-there kiss. A tingle that felt like static electricity or something. A strangeness that was disturbing, anyway.

So Finn backed away fast. He put on his most charming smile, as if that kiss was nothing out of the ordinary for two friends, and turned away to pick up the tray on the table.

'Call me,' he said. 'If you need any help in the night. With Beanie *or* Ben.'

CHAPTER SIX

FINN HAD BEEN gone for many hours. All afternoon and now the evening was ticking on. He'd had urgent meetings that needed to happen face to face. The police apparently had some information for him. Jude and executives from his television show's channel wanted a word and senior staff at the animal hospital were also asking for his attention.

There'd been so much going on out here in the mountains that Hazel had been too busy to wonder what information the police had discovered or why Finn hadn't made contact to say he would be so late back. And she'd been far too busy to let her mind keep drifting back to what had kept her awake for rather too much of the night. Not that she was feeling tired from the lack of sleep, however. If anything, there was a curious source of energy to be found in thinking about it.

A kind of buzz that could be turned on

repeatedly. Every time Hazel touched a fin-
gertip to her lips, in fact. Just ever so lightly.
With exactly the same pressure that Finn's
lips had touched her own last night. Not that
it had meant anything, of course. He'd probably been intending to kiss her on the cheek,
like he had when he'd told her that he loved
her, as a friend whose help he appreciated,
and he'd just missed his mark. And, even
if it had been deliberate, it certainly hadn't
registered as a passionate kind of kiss but...

But it was delicious to remember it.

And it was just as well she was so busy
she couldn't spend any time letting her heart
try and convince her head that there was any
significance to it at all.

Finn's housekeeper, Sandra, had been here
for most of the day to help with caring for
Ellie, which was just as well, because her
husband had arrived this afternoon with the
neglected donkey in their float and the farrier
had arrived not long after that to tackle the
sadly overdue footcare that had taken several
hours to complete.

They'd all left a while ago now, but Hazel
had needed to feed and bathe baby Ellie and
get her settled, she'd given Kiara a quick
phone call to share an update on the newly
rescued donkey and now she was rummag-

ing in the pantry to find treats, like carrots and apples, that she could mix into the mash she planned to make from feed pellets that had been delivered along with the straw she'd used to line the stable. Sandra had left meat and vegetables roasting in the oven for when Finn finally came back and it would be nice to set a table out on the veranda perhaps, where they could share the meal.

So, there was still plenty to think about and there was no excuse to keep remembering that kiss when Hazel carried the bucket of mash out to the stables in one hand, with the baby monitor handset in the other. Seeing her beloved red van coming down the driveway and knowing that Finn was behind the wheel *was* an excuse to let her brain wander back to that touch of his lips on hers but, even before the vehicle came to a halt, Hazel found herself thinking about something very different.

Something that wasn't delicious at all.

She'd thought Finn had looked wrecked that night she'd gone to his apartment, with his shadowed jaw and finger rumpled hair. She'd seen him look so vulnerable when he'd confessed how hopeless he felt trying to look after a baby. And, just yesterday morning, he'd been so obviously exhausted it seemed to have stripped yet another layer from what she was used to seeing in Finn but what Hazel was looking at now, as he climbed out of the van, was a combination of all of those impressions. This was a person who was possibly completely shattered. A person she would always be there for even if he was never aware of how deeply she cared about him.

'Oh, my God, Finn…' Hazel's grip on the bucket loosened. 'What's happened?'

His eyes looked so dark in a face that was too pale.

'The DNA results are back. There's no doubt that I'm related closely enough to Elena to be her grandfather.' Finn was pushing his hair back from his forehead yet again. 'They call it the "grandparentage index value".' He gave an ironic huff of sound. 'I've always revelled in getting a high score in any tests I've done but, this time… I'm still trying to get my head around it.'

Hazel nodded. 'Of course you are.' She tightened her grip on the handle of the bucket she hadn't quite dropped. 'Come with me for a minute. I've got something to do in the stables.'

Finn's nod was almost absent-minded as

he followed her. 'You need some help? Did the donkey arrive, then?'

'Yes. I've got a bit of a treat for her supper before being left for the first night somewhere new and scary. It's been a big day.'

'Is she okay? Did the farrier come?'

'Yes. And yes. The farrier was amazing. The poor thing could barely walk off the float but he's managed to create almost normal looking hooves. He even had a portable X-ray machine to check the position of the pedal bones before he started. The feet are still too sore to move much at the moment, so I've got her shut in the stable on deep straw, but she'll be able to get out into the paddock in the next few days.'

Hazel kept talking as she led the way to the stables, hoping to give Finn a moment's distraction from his crisis. A moment of calm before a new storm, perhaps, and there was no better place to find calmness than in the company of a donkey.

Sure enough, Finn walked through the straw and began stroking the small grey donkey and scratching her neck just below an enormous ear. The donkey leaned against him and rubbed her head up and down to encourage the petting to continue. Hazel could almost feel some of his stress evaporating, which was exactly what she'd been hoping would happen. This was the first gift she'd been able to think of offering Finn but it felt like she was getting just as much pleasure from its acceptance. Especially when Finn smiled at her like that.

'Friendly little guy, isn't he?'

'He's a girl,' Hazel reminded him. 'Probably around five or six years old and it's possible she's never had her feet properly trimmed. Her elderly owner loved her but had no idea how to look after a donkey and now she's been taken into a rest home and the RSPCA got called in to help with various pets.'

'Has she got a name?'

'Isabella.' Hazel moved closer with the bucket and the donkey lowered its head to sniff the contents. Finn was still smiling as he watched the curious donkey swing her ears forwards but then it faded rapidly.

'The DNA results were just one part of the worst day I think I've ever had,' he told Hazel. 'I had a journalist hounding me for my comment on Shannon being seen out with another man. Some celebrity chef. It seems like she's backdating the end of our relationship to a point that means she was never involved with a grandfather.'

'She said that?' Hazel was appalled. 'She's spread your private business on social media?'

'No. The official wording is that we've both moved on in an amicable separation but it's only a matter of time until the news is out there. I'm going to have to make some major changes in my life.'

For a long moment, Finn stood there silently, still stroking the donkey, and then he let his breath out in a long sigh. 'What was it that you wanted me to help with? Isabella doesn't seem unwell. She's scoffing whatever's in that bucket.'

'She's fine. I've already given her some more painkillers for her feet. She won't need anything more until morning.'

'Oh…' Finn was frowning. 'I thought that's why you asked me to come out here. To help with the donkey.'

'No…' Hazel's smile was gentle. 'I thought some donkey time might help *you*.'

She was holding Finn's gaze as she spoke so she could see the moment he understood not only why she'd brought him out to the stable but that she'd wanted to help because she genuinely cared about him. About who he really was, not the competent colleague or TV star or even the unexpected grandparent, but the person who was hidden beneath all those layers. The person he'd been right from when he was a small boy and the things in his life that had shaped him into the man he was today.

A man who was still looking shattered.

'Your amazing Sandra made dinner that's keeping warm in the oven. I'm guessing you haven't eaten much today?'

Finn shook his head. 'I haven't been remotely hungry. I haven't told you what the rest of the afternoon threw at me. What the police have found out. About my…about Ellie's mother…'

It was the first time he'd called the baby 'Ellie', Hazel realised. And had he been about to call the baby's mother his daughter? No wonder he was rubbing at his forehead now, as if it might help with shellshocked thoughts that were bouncing around in his head.

'I'm willing to bet you'll feel hungry as soon as you get a whiff of that roast beef and crispy potatoes,' she assured Finn. 'There's even a jug of real gravy that didn't come out of a packet.'

Did he realise that she was offering another pause? A reprieve from having to juggle the onslaught of more than one huge life change that had been thrown at him in the space of a single afternoon? Hazel was more than happy to listen to whatever he wanted to tell her and offer whatever comfort she could, but she was also happy to simply be with him because she knew that it was always better not to be alone when life seemed too difficult. Ben the first had taught her that lesson.

And maybe Finn had also learned that lesson a long time ago because he draped his arm over Hazel's shoulders as they walked back to the house. A casual gesture of friendship, perhaps, but she knew the memory of this touch would get filed in the same special place as last night's kiss. Along with his words.

'Asking you to stay was probably the best idea I've ever had, Hazel. And, you know what…?'

'What?'

She looked up in time to catch the beginning of a smile that grew wide enough to suggest that Finn was gladly accepting the offer of some time out.

'I'm *starving*,' he said.

There was a formal dining room in the house with a gorgeous antique table big enough to seat at least twelve people that had been included in the furnishings when he'd purchased this property, but it didn't occur to

Finn to suggest using it tonight. Sitting on antique, spindle-back chairs to eat at the old work table in the kitchen was not just the easiest thing to do—it felt…right. As if he and Hazel did this all the time because it was comfortable and familiar.

Because it was home.

There were interruptions to the casual meal, with Ben needing help to go outside and Ellie needing to be fed and changed and settled into her bassinette, but it didn't matter that the food got a bit too cool or that there was a long gap between the main course and the wonderful, gooey chocolate pudding that Sandra had made. They shared what needed to be done because that felt just as natural as eating in the kitchen. They were a team, weren't they?

And amazingly—given what Hazel had said about how superficial his lifestyle was and that he himself was fake—it seemed that she cared about him. She wasn't here simply because he'd bribed her by offering a place for Ben to recuperate and an opportunity to rescue a neglected donkey.

She really cared, didn't she? Putting two and two together and realising that Hazel had deliberately taken him out to the stables when he'd arrived home in such a state because she knew that being with, and touching, a gentle animal like Isabella could make him feel better had given Finn a weird sort of melting sensation deep in his gut. When was the last time someone had cared enough not only to wonder how he was really feeling but to try and make things better for him?

Probably not since Ellie.

Because he'd never allowed anyone to see how he was really feeling?

It wasn't as though he'd consciously taken down any barriers for Hazel, though. They simply...weren't there... Because he'd known all along that Hazel was the friend he could trust the most, which was why he'd been so desperate for her help with this crisis? Why he still needed her to be close?

It was getting really late by the time Finn poured the last of the bottle of wine they'd shared with their dinner into their glasses.

'We should probably go to bed,' Hazel said. And then she caught Finn's gaze and, to his astonishment, her cheeks flooded with colour as she ducked her head. 'Oh... I didn't mean... I just meant it was late...'

Her reaction was charming, but it was also poignant. Had people in her past, like that jerk Michael, made her doubt how attractive she was to the point that she might think a first move on her part might be unwelcome? Not that Finn had the head space for anything more than a flash of remembering the unexpected attraction he'd felt for Hazel himself because he was still thinking about the way she had revealed how much she cared about him and how that had opened a space where so many other memories had been locked away.

'I need to tell you about Ellie,' he said quictly. 'And about what the police found out.'

He could feel how still Hazel became. How intently she was already listening.

But where to begin? Finn closed his eyes, letting his breath out in a sigh, as he failed to find a logical starting point and then he heard Hazel's soft words.

'You loved her.'

'I reckon she saved my life.' Finn opened his eyes. 'We were in the same class at high school when we were fifteen and we were the kids that everyone felt sorry for. Elena, because her father was known for being vicious and me...well, I was the kid no one had ever wanted, or not for very long, anyway. I started at that school after I'd been moved on to yet another foster home and it was only a matter of time until I got into enough trouble to get sent somewhere else—like juvenile detention, maybe. Ellie caught me one day trying to set fire to the school shed and she told me how stupid I was. That, if I wanted to get anywhere in life, I'd better learn to stay out of trouble.'

He let his eyes drift shut again because these were memories that, even after all this time, still hurt.

'I get it,' Hazel said. 'Not that I did stuff to get into trouble, but it was too hard to hide from what the other kids dished out.'

Finn's eyes snapped open. 'You got bullied?'

'I was the fat kid.' Hazel shrugged. 'Easy target.' She gave her head a tiny shake as if she was done talking about it. 'I wish I'd had someone in my corner like you did.'

Finn almost told her that he wished *he'd* been that someone in her corner. How crazy was that? Instead of saying anything, however, he touched her hand in a simple gesture of connection. She understood the despair of feeling unwanted and that connection meant he didn't need barriers with this woman.

'We had two years together,' he told her. 'And we pushed each other to do well at school because we were both going to conquer the world as soon as we were old enough to escape. We were the best of friends and then we fell in love and then…and then she just disappeared. Her father told me she'd been offered a job in Sydney and what was the point of girls finishing high school anyway and her mother…well, she wouldn't even speak to me. And… I never knew why she'd gone without even saying goodbye. Until now… I think her mother must have arranged it and warned her never to come back because her father would have killed her if he'd known that…that…'

'That she was pregnant…' Hazel finished for him.

Finn nodded. 'The police found a record of Beanie's birth. Isolated outback town. No father mentioned but the mother's name was Jamie Ferrari.'

Hazel's breath caught. '*Jamie?* Ellie named her baby after you?'

The prickle at the back of Finn's eyes couldn't be simply blinked away. Not when Hazel was thinking exactly what he'd thought.

'She loved you, too,' she whispered. 'And it was precious to her that she had your baby. Did she have to give her up for adoption?'

Finn shook his head. 'She still had Jamie with her when she died ten years ago and she was a single mother with no known family so

Jamie went into foster care because she was only eight.' He had to swallow hard. 'Talk about history repeating itself.'

The tears that had been forming got big enough to escape his eyes and somehow, Finn wasn't the least bit surprised to see that Hazel was also crying. And it was as natural as anything else that evening that they both leaned close enough to put their arms around each other and stayed in that hug for the longest time.

'You were so right,' he said, finally pulling back so that he could see her face. 'About me being shallow.'

He could feel Hazel taking a quick breath to say something but he didn't let her.

'When Ellie vanished,' he continued quickly, 'I was devastated. And then I was angry. And then I made up my mind that nobody was ever going to do anything like that to me again. I was going to work my butt off and make enough money because that meant the security to do whatever I wanted and that I was going to become *somebody*. Somebody important enough to be special.'

To be loved, he almost added. But he didn't say it aloud because it was too personal. A longing that had been buried deep in his heart for so long it was too hard to share. And he'd got lost somewhere along the way, anyway, so that money and fame and everything that Hazel quite rightly deemed less important in life had taken over. But it seemed that he didn't have to say it aloud in any case, because he could see what looked like complete understanding in Hazel's eyes.

'You are somebody special,' she said. 'And, because you're so well known, your daughter knew where to find you. And I think Jamie will come back because you have something very important in common.'

'What? That we're related? I've never met her. I didn't even know she existed.'

'You both knew Ellie. *Your* Ellie. And you both loved her. You had a baby with her. And Jamie named *her* baby after her. And…' Hazel reached up to brush a tear from Finn's cheek. 'And I couldn't have been more wrong. You're not shallow, Finn. You know exactly what matters most in life—I think you've just been scared of trusting it.'

She got to her feet and held out her hand. 'It's been quite a day, hasn't it? We both need some sleep before Beanie wakes up again.'

Finn took hold of Hazel's hand as he got up. He found he didn't want to let it go when they reached his bedroom door.

'Stay with me?' he asked quietly. 'Please?'

Oh, help… Did she think he was asking for sex? He wasn't. He just wanted to be close enough to feel her warmth and hear her breathing. They could both sleep with their clothes on, but he *needed* to be near her right now. He'd never get to sleep by himself and he didn't want to lie awake for the rest of the night.

'Just…just for company?' he added. 'You're right—it's been quite a day…'

He couldn't read her expression exactly, but it was something soft. A bit like the way she'd looked when she'd suggested he went to the stables with her. That look of caring.

Of a kind of love that was the opposite of anything shallow. Or fake.

Hazel wasn't letting go of his hand, either. Until they both kicked off their shoes and lay down and Finn pulled the duvet over them as Hazel curled up in his arms. He'd never been this close to someone this soft, he realised, as he let his head rest on her shoulder—exhaustion already pulling him towards the blessed oblivion of sleep. Or someone so warm—in every sense of the word. Was this so different because it might be the first time he'd ever invited a woman into his bed for something other than sex? How odd was it that this actually felt more intimate?

More…*real.*
It felt…
Well…it felt like home…

Hazel stayed very, very still in Finn's arms. And she tried, very, very hard, not to fall asleep because she didn't want to miss a second of feeling like this—as if she was the one person that Finn had trusted to tell his story to. The one person he needed to be with him so that he could feel safe enough to sleep. She listened to his breathing as it grew quieter and slower and she could feel the thump of his heartbeat slowing as well as he slid into unconsciousness.

Was he dreaming about Ellie? His first—and his only   true love? Hazel could only begin to imagine how bewildered and heartbroken he must have been when she simply vanished from his life and, when she couldn't fight sleep any longer, she dreamed of a youth who'd pinned his hopes on being able to buy safety, and even love, if only he had enough money and status and her own heart had to be breaking as she slept because she could feel the dampness of tears on the pillow when she opened her eyes at some point before dawn.

She wasn't the only one awake. Hazel had

turned in her sleep and she was facing Finn now, instead of having him pressed against her back. His face was only a few inches from her own so the eye contact felt as intimate as a kiss. The intensity of it made Hazel catch her breath, which was when she realised that her breasts were pushed firmly against Finn's chest and…oh, help…her leg was hooked over his and it didn't matter that they were both still dressed because she could feel that Finn was becoming aroused— probably because of the way she was draped all over him—and, oh, man… Hazel needed to find a reason to slip from this bed before Finn found an excuse to move away himself. It would be really great, she thought, if baby Ellie would start crying, like right *now*…

But there was no sound other than the quiet sigh of their breathing. Finn had his arm across the pillow over her head and, just as Hazel had decided she could say she'd better go and check on Ben and/or Isabella, he moved his hand to stroke her hair and any coherent thought evaporated before it could become speech. And then Finn cupped the side of her head and came closer and Hazel was expecting another gentle brush of his lips on hers, a friendly sort of insignificant kiss that could easily morph into an exit strategy, but as soon as she felt his touch it was very obvious that this kiss was going to be nothing at all like the one they'd shared on the veranda the other night.

This…was as real as a kiss could get.

As powerful as a taste of distilled desire and, with the first glide of Finn's tongue against her own, she could feel an edge that was almost dangerous—something wild that had yet to be unleashed. And maybe it shouldn't be unleashed, because it might be only on her side of this physical equation and…

And Finn was looking at her again and it felt as if he was seeing her for the first time ever and he was looking…astonished…

'Where on earth did you learn to kiss like that?' His voice was almost a growl.

'Like what…? It was just a kiss…'

'Are you *kidding*? That's *just* a kiss for you?'

'I'm a bit rusty. It's been a while.' Hazel could feel her lips curling into a smile because she could hear more than amazement in his tone. She could hear desire. His as well as her own. She could feel it, too. A tension that was building rapidly into something that could very well explode.

'Hazel…'

'Mmm?'

Finn blinked very slowly. 'This might sound weird because I know we've only ever been friends but…but I really want to make love to you.'

Hazel's mouth suddenly felt too dry to make it easy to say anything.

'You can say "no",' Finn added softly. 'It's probably the last thing you'd want, right?'

'Are you *kidding*?'

That tension, on Hazel's side, had already started a countdown to the point where all control would be forfeited. She could only hope that baby Ellie would choose this night to sleep as long as possible after the dawning of a new day. She was the one who was closing that gap between herself and Finn this time and her words were no more than the ghost of a whisper.

'It's the *only* thing I want…'

CHAPTER SEVEN

'SHE'S SMILING AT ME.'

'No way…she's never smiled at *me*.'

'Well, she smiled at me. Look…she's doing it again…'

Hazel put the still sizzling pan of bacon, eggs and mushrooms onto the metal trivet on the kitchen table with a clatter, moving swiftly to peer over Finn's shoulder, leaning close enough for his hair to tickle her ear and for every cell in her body to respond to that feather-light contact with a delicious combination of both desire and blissful satisfaction.

The way those same cells had responded, only an hour or two ago, to every touch given and received in Finn's bed this morning when they'd made love for the first time.

When Hazel's world had changed for ever.

She had to close her eyes for a heartbeat now and simply take a breath. Nothing could ever be the same, could it? Maybe…okay, probably, this new level of her relationship with Finn wasn't going to last. Maybe, for Finn, it was nothing more than a physical connection and maybe she'd never find anyone else that she could feel this way about but something in Hazel had changed for ever.

Because she knew what it felt like to love—and be loved—like that.

And it was adding a whole new, amazing layer to what was currently happening in this kitchen. It had been Finn who'd given his granddaughter her breakfast bottle as Hazel was cooking and he'd remembered to burp her against his shoulder when she was finished. Hazel had been laughing at how proud Finn was of Ellie's ability to burp so loudly but then he'd made the announcement and...

And now it was a moment that was...huge.

Almost seven-week-old Elena Ferrari was smiling and smiling, looking overjoyed at this newfound talent, and her grandfather was smiling back at her and making the sort of nonsense sounds that even the most intelligent adults used to communicate with babies they had totally fallen in love with. And then he looked up to make sure Hazel was sharing the moment and she could see by the way he was blinking back a tear or two that he was just as aware as she was of how huge this was. Maybe he was even feeling some of the lingering magic of their lovemaking adding its own layer to this new bond between them.

Hazel had to blink back the mistiness in her own eyes as her heart overflowed with its own joy in this moment. It was very close to being overwhelming, in fact, because there was nothing she would want to change about her life in this tiny pocket of time. Why would she? She had everything anyone could possibly want. For an odd nanosecond Hazel could imagine looking down on this scene from a long, long way away. She would see a gorgeous house in a beautiful part of the world, a kitchen that was made for family meals and laughter with the aroma of delicious food filling the room, a dog who was lying on the floor nearby—his tail gently thumping the mat—a baby who was smiling for the first time that they knew of and a man who had just become her lover. A man who was a very different person from the man who'd been so shocked that his celebrity lifestyle was about to implode.

But this was the *real* James Finlay right here. The man who had bonded with the daughter of the daughter of his own that he'd never known existed and this tiny baby had broken a barrier around his heart. That was the most important thing that had happened since baby Ellie had landed in their lives but in its wake, by some miracle, Hazel had been allowed into that inner space where she could properly meet the man she had fallen totally in love with. He'd shared things she was quite sure that nobody else knew about and, while they might have been unwanted by their peer group for different reasons as they'd grown up, there was a connection there that Hazel had never found before.

Maybe she'd always been able to see a glimpse of that man and that was why she'd had that instant crush on her employer that she'd had to try and quell ever since she'd started work at the Coogee Beach Animal Hospital. It had made no sense to be so attracted to someone like *Call the Vet* star Dr Finn who would only ever have someone like Shannon Summers as a partner but she'd never been able to make those feelings go away completely and now she knew why.

Her love for Finn was also very real.

The kind that could last a lifetime.

And there was no hiding from that any longer. Not that she was about to scare Finn by telling him how she felt. Not when they were such new lovers and every moment together, especially in bed, had an edge of newborn, miraculous fragility that was too precious to risk damaging in any way. She held his gaze a heartbeat longer, though, the way lovers were allowed to do, so that she could feel the joy of *his* joy.

And to feel a perfection that could never last more than a moment because something would change any second now. Maybe Ellie would stop smiling or Ben would stop wagging his tail or Finn would simply look away or…yep…the toaster popping was enough. But it didn't matter because Hazel knew there would be another moment before too long and it would be just as good—maybe even better.

'There's our toast. Would you like butter or avocado on it?'

'Avo, please.' Finn was smiling down at Ellie again. 'Nom-nom-nom. Avo and bacon and eggs. The breakfast of kings, that's what it is, Beanie. Who knew that our Hazel was such a brilliant cook?'

Our Hazel.

She liked that. She liked it so much it was almost another one of those moments all by itself.

* * *

Finn had always known that life had turning points that you could look back on and realise that everything had changed. For ever.

Like that day when he'd been on the verge of deciding that life simply wasn't worth living and maybe he was going to do something about that after he'd torched the school shed and Ellie had appeared from nowhere and torn strips off him for being so dumb and…it had felt as if someone actually cared whether or not he was breathing.

Or the day he'd faced television cameras for the first time as both his life and career took a new direction and he'd loved it because it made him feel important and he suspected it was going to make him a lot richer and they were both the things that mattered the most, weren't they?

Finding Beanie in the pet carrier in the waiting room was the latest turning point and one that was most definitely going to change everything for the rest of his life. He had a family member for the first time ever and she was totally dependent on him.

But was that dramatic moment really the latest turning point?

What about that night he'd made love to Hazel Davidson for the first time?

His gaze slid sideways to where Hazel was sitting in the passenger seat of her van. Finn was driving, because he was enjoying the novelty of using manual gears after only driving automatic cars for so long. The transmission of this vintage vehicle couldn't be considered smooth, of course, but the muscle memory of using the clutch and shifting the gear stick had been easy to tap into and... it was *fun*.

So was making love to Hazel.

The way their friendship had expanded to include this kind of intimacy would have been unthinkable even a couple of weeks ago and yet it seemed like it had always been meant to happen. The way Ellie had been meant to find him that day at school and change his life for ever? No...sleeping with Hazel wasn't that much of a turning point. It couldn't be, because trusting another person to that extent—even someone like Hazel was a mistake he was never going to make again. Did he need to make sure that Hazel understood? So that she wouldn't get hurt by hoping for something that was never going to happen?

This was about friendship, that was all. And about the unexpected bonus of such great sex...

As if she'd read his thoughts, Hazel ducked her head as if she was a little embarrassed, but she was smiling as she turned to look into the back of the van where Ben was lying in a crate.

'Is he okay?' Finn asked. 'He's not getting too bumped around, is he?'

'He seems happy enough.' But Finn could hear the anxious note in Hazel's voice.

'I think he's doing well,' he said reassuringly. 'The incision's healing beautifully and he's not needing painkillers any longer. It's only a matter of time before he starts trying to put some weight on that leg.'

'So you don't think I need to X-ray him? Will I be wasting clinic time and resources?'

'Not at all.' Finn threw her a smile. 'I think it's exactly what you should do to give you peace of mind about his recovery.'

Plus, it meant that he had the pleasure of Hazel's company for a trip into the city for appointments and Sandra had been only too happy to step in to babysit Beanie.

The reminder of why Hazel was coming with him and that he'd shamelessly used Ben to persuade Hazel to stay with him so he wasn't entirely alone in dealing with a life crisis made him change his mind about that latest potential turning point in his life because it eased his concern that his control of this surprising new level of friendship might be at risk. Hazel knew him well enough to know that it wasn't going to continue for ever, didn't she? Wasn't that partly why she'd accused him of being like Shannon? Being superficial? She knew that Finn didn't *do* relationships like that—or not with women, anyway. Or pets, for that matter, but Ben the dog and Isabella the donkey were also only temporary additions to his lifestyle—a kind of package deal that came with Hazel.

He'd certainly never expected to have a close relationship with a child, either, but he didn't have any choice about that now and, with more than a week of it under his belt, he was starting to get used to it. There were moments he was actually happy it had happened, in fact—like the other morning when Beanie had smiled at him and it had melted his heart. Finn found himself smiling as he remembered that moment, shifting down a gear at the same time to take a sharp curve in the road more slowly.

Making love to Hazel had also been surprisingly memorable, mind you, and not simply because the desire to do so had seemed to come from nowhere with such unexpected strength to it. Or that Hazel had seemed to want the physical connection as much as he did. No…the real revelation had come later. Could it really be that he had totally forgotten what *real* breasts felt like? Everything about Hazel's body was soft and delicious and, best of all, she was the most generous lover in her response and initiation of everything they'd played with on several occasions now. He'd never felt so appreciated in bed.

Loved, even?

No…he wasn't about to go down that track. That was the route to losing perspective. Control, even.

He was confident that he and Hazel were on the same page, here, although a conversation to confirm that, before too long, would probably be a good idea. They were friends who, thanks to Ben needing a place to recuperate, were sharing what was a kind of temporary, forced isolation from the world and normal life, apart from taking turns to go into the city for work commitments or, like today, travelling in together because they both had things they needed to do.

Hazel was going to run a morning surgery session and X-ray Ben's leg and he had an appointment with Jude and TV station executives involved with *Call the Vet* to discuss upcoming shooting schedules, a consultation for a specialist orthopaedic opinion on a dog and an appointment with Social Services early this afternoon. Thinking of those appointments made it easy to forget about a conversation with Hazel that really wasn't a priority. They were clearly both quite happy with what was happening and maybe talking about it could change things.

Finn didn't want to change anything. Not yet, anyway. And, if it wasn't broken, it didn't need fixing, did it?

'I think I might go and collect my own car after my meeting this afternoon,' he told Hazel. 'Surely the paparazzi will have given up staking out my apartment building by now.' He smiled at her again. 'Not that I'm not enjoying driving this relic, but it would be rather nice to reclaim a bit of normality.'

It was only someone like Dr Finn, TV star, who would consider driving something like the latest and most expensive model from Porsche to be normal but Hazel could understand why he was looking forward to driving a vehicle he loved. She found herself wondering what other parts of his life he might be desperate to reclaim. Living in that sleek penthouse apartment with its stunning sea views? Repairing his relationship with Shannon Summers yet again?

Hazel swallowed hard as she pushed that thought away. Deep down, she knew perfectly well that this fantasy she was living wasn't going to last for ever but...she could dream for a bit, couldn't she? Hope was such a seductive emotion and it had been a very long time since she'd felt it was close enough to touch.

Hearing her phone ring was a welcome reprieve from any seed of doubt that was trying to implant itself in her mind although seeing the name on the screen created a new worry. Kiara wouldn't ring at this time of day unless something was wrong.

'Hey...what's up? It's not Bunji, is it?'

'No...she's okay. Not that I've had time to do much with her yet. I'm on my own and there's too much to do. Anyway, I've had a call from the police. They're at a residence in Glenbrook. Elderly person's been found dead and there's a cat...'

Hazel turned to Finn a few moments later. 'Did you notice where that last motorway exit was for?'

'Warrimoo.'

Kiara had heard his response. 'So you're already heading into the city?'

'Into Coogee...' Hazel bit her lip. 'I guess it's not that far to take a detour to Glenbrook.' She turned back to Finn. 'Would we have time to rescue a cat? Owner's been found dead and the police want the cat taken care of. The local vet put them on to Two Tails but Kiara can't leave the refuge right now. Her specialty's rehoming dogs, anyway, but no one else seems available to pick this cat up so if I can go she'll take it.'

'Sure.' Finn glanced at his watch. 'I've got plenty of time before my first appointment.'

Hazel ended the call, having scribbled down address details, and then she used her phone to find out how far it was to the exit they would need to take.

'Kiara can never say no, even if she doesn't have the time or space. But it sounds like this cat needs a vet, anyway. The police officer at the scene says it won't let anyone near it and it's making funny noises.'

It was a bizarre scene they arrived at a short time later. There were police cars and a hearse parked outside the house and neighbours gathered on the footpath to watch the events that had disrupted their ordinary, suburban normality this morning. The arrival of a small, bright red, vintage van only added to their interest.

'Oh, my God…' Hazel heard someone say. 'Isn't that Dr Finn? From…you know… *Call the Vet*?'

'He'll be here to rescue Mittens,' someone else said. 'Look, he's got a carrier box. And that's just the sort of thing he does, isn't it?'

Well…not quite, Hazel thought, but it seemed he was branching out today. They went into the house to find the funeral home people preparing to remove the body from the house.

'You can't really complain,' a police officer was saying. 'To die in your sleep when you're ninety-four is not a bad way to go, is it?' She turned as Finn and Hazel came in. 'Are you from the animal rescue place?'

'Yes.'

'Cat's over there. Hiding beside the chest of drawers in the bedroom.'

Hazel peered into the dark space between the chest of drawers and the wall and made soothing sounds, reaching in to stroke the cat, but it hissed at her and shrank further back, making odd chirruping noises.

'I'll find my torch. Maybe it's injured.'

Finn knelt down and looked into the space. 'Hey…' he murmured. 'What's going on, puss? Things are a bit weird around here this morning, aren't they?'

The cat wasn't hissing. Finn kept up his reassuring conversation as he carefully reached into the gap and the sound Hazel heard from the cat sounded like a relieved miaow. One that might even morph into purring?

'She likes you.'

'She's a nice cat,' Finn said. 'A Birman, I think. She's very fluffy and she's got little white socks.'

'Possibly why she's got the original name of "Mittens".' Hazel was smiling as she handed him her phone with the torch app activated. 'Poor thing. She must be really scared at what's happening. Let's get her into the carrier. It'll be a nice, safe space.'

'Um…' Finn was staring into the now well illuminated gap. 'Maybe not just yet.'

'Why not?' Hazel leaned in to see what he was seeing. She had to press her head against his shoulder to get a good view. 'Oh…'

'Mmm… That's a kitten born in the last five minutes, I'd say.'

The tiny creature was stretching miniature legs and had its mouth opening in silent mews. It was an unusual colour with big black spots on a mainly white body.

'So *cute*,' Hazel whispered.

'I don't think she's finished yet,' Finn whispered back. He caught her gaze. 'I think we'd better put our midwife hats on. Looks like she's having contractions.'

'Have you got time? What about that appointment with the TV people?'

'I can let them know I'll be late.' One corner of his mouth lifted in a lopsided smile. 'I think babies are becoming my thing.'

Oh…it wasn't just this baby animal that was impossibly adorable, was it? How could you not love a man who was prepared to dismiss everything in favour of bringing helpless kittens safely into the world?

It was nearly an hour later that Finn picked up each of four tiny kittens to place them, with their mother, in the carrier, which Hazel had made cosy with a handknitted rug from a chair in the living room of the house.

'I'm sure she would want her cat to have something that smells familiar with her,' Hazel said. 'She looks like a much-loved pet. I'd better let Kiara know there's more than just the cat that will need rehoming.'

'She'll need watching for the next few days to make sure she's coping with the kittens.' Finn had one of the newborns in the palm of his hand. 'Didn't you say your friend is a bit too busy at the moment?' He held the kitten up, closing his eyes as he very gently touched noses with it. Then he opened his eyes and smiled at Hazel. 'Maybe we should take them all home with us.'

Hazel smiled back. She knew it was a misty smile that was probably inappropriate for a friendship that might include benefits but hadn't earned the status of a significant relationship by any means, but she couldn't stop herself. 'Because babies are your thing now?'

'Temporarily, anyway,' Finn agreed. 'Might as well go with the flow.'

The 'flow' was moving more swiftly than Finn had realised. And the direction of the current was changing unexpectedly as well. Maybe it had had something to do with delivering those kittens that morning. Or possibly, it was due to the fast-paced atmosphere of the meeting he had with the television station executives later that day where ideas were being thrown around about how they could use Finn's popularity to take the show in new directions. Perhaps Dr Finn could go travelling to do stories on unusual animals in different countries? Or, as Jude suggested, he could get involved in rescues that could be with domestic or wild animals. Someone else said that they were fielding requests for him to make guest appearances on both cooking and quiz shows. Finn was wondering, for the first time, if branching out from being the star of a reality veterinary show was really the direction he wanted his career to go in.

Another unexpected swirl in the current of that flow appeared when he got Hazel to drive him to his apartment building when she was ready to head home, with Ben back in his crate and a glowing report card on his healing fracture and Mittens with her kittens in the carrier beside him. He would take his own car to the meeting with Social Services and then follow her out of the city.

'Stop here,' he directed, a little way from his building. He shook his head only a short time after Hazel had parked discreetly. 'See that guy? The one in the leather jacket, leaning on his car?'

'Yes…oh…that's a camera bag on his roof, isn't it?'

'Yeah…and even if I sneak in through the back and get into the basement garage, I'll still have to drive out onto the street right there, by the front entrance and my car's a bit too easy to recognise. He'd be on my tail instantly and the last thing we want is someone following us out of town.'

'Mmm…'

'Keep going,' Finn told her. 'There's a car dealership a block or two away.'

'You're going to rent something?'

'I might *buy* something.' As the words emerged, they felt like the right thing to be saying. 'A Porsche isn't exactly the kind of car you want to be strapping a baby seat into, is it? I'm thinking it might be time to look at, oh, I don't know…an SUV, maybe?'

It wasn't that Finn was really expecting to be adopting his grandchild and bringing her up but he fully intended to be a significant part of her life and he could keep two cars, couldn't he? An SUV for times with Beanie and the Porsche for his own playtime. He glanced at his watch.

'We've got thirty minutes. If I pick one, they might even be able to have it ready for me by the time the meeting's finished.' He grinned at Hazel. 'Come with me?'

'What, to pick the colour of your car or be the taxi to your meeting?'

'Well, I'd certainly welcome your opinion on colour but…' Finn's smile faded. 'But I think you should come to the meeting with me, anyway.'

'What? With the people from Social Services? Why?'

'Because you're just as involved in Bean-

ie's care as I am so you should know what's
going on and I'm sure Margaret would love
to meet you.'

Of course she would. Who wouldn't love
Hazel? And who wouldn't approve of the
combination of Hazel and Finn caring for a
vulnerable baby? If he'd ever thought of settling down and having a family of his own,
then someone like Hazel would be exactly
who he'd choose as a partner.

No…not someone like Hazel.

Just… Hazel.

Good grief…where had that thought come
from? When only hours ago he'd reassured
himself that he was completely in control of
what was going on between them and that
they were both on the same page? Finn felt
like he'd been ambushed by something he'd
been avoiding his whole adult life. Hazel
would probably be as alarmed as he was by
the idea so he owed it to her to dismiss it
once and for all. Finn cleared his throat.

'Margaret's great,' he added quickly.
'She's passionate about the kids and babies
that she's involved with and she's probably
in her sixties, I guess, so she's seen it all before.' Hunching down in the passenger seat
as they drove past the photographer waiting
outside the apartment block was just the dis-

traction he needed to entirely dismiss that weird idea he'd had of choosing Hazel to be the mother of the children he was never planning to have.

'He didn't see you,' Hazel assured him.

'Good.' Finn let his breath out in a sigh as he straightened up. 'I'm getting to the point when I'd prefer to get on with making this public so I'm hoping they're going to find Jamie soon. We don't want to scare her off because having her involved will make things a lot more straightforward. We can do whatever needs doing to help her look after her baby but, if that's not going to happen, it would be easier if she was part of an adoption process that would let me do it.'

'You're planning to *adopt* Beanie?' Hazel's swift glance was astonished. 'You'd bring her up yourself?'

'If that's what it takes,' Finn said. 'I need to protect her.' He pulled in a deep breath. 'I'm not going to let her grow up thinking that she wasn't wanted.'

Like he had been…

Maybe like her own mother had felt…?

This was where it would stop. History was not going to repeat itself yet again.

Hazel was looking at him again as she stopped for a red light before turning into the street where the car dealership was located. He could feel that she was watching him. And, even though—for some reason— he didn't want to meet her gaze, he knew it was one of those soft looks. That he'd impressed her in some way. That she liked what she was seeing. It gave him an odd curl of something in his gut. Pride? Maybe. It was something nice, anyway, but he didn't want too much of it.

Because it was an emotional gift from someone else and it was better not to accept them. Because they couldn't be trusted. Sometimes they got taken away again. Sometimes, people just took them and walked out of your life. For ever.

But this was Hazel and, deep down, Finn knew she would never walk out on anybody she cared about. Because she knew what it was like to not be wanted, too. Not that he'd pushed her to talk about how badly she'd been bullied at school but it was easy to see that her confidence came through caring for others and that she shrank back if the spotlight was turned on her. Like the way she'd been flustered when she'd seen something in his face that told her he was thinking something nice about her. About how much fun it was to make love to her…

Oh…that did it. If she was still looking at him when he turned his head, she might have to accept an emotional gift from *him*. But even as the thought formed the light was changing and the van was moving again. And Finn had to admit it was kind of a relief to have their interaction head back to something entirely platonic.

'Red,' Hazel said firmly. 'Like the colour of this van. You can't go wrong with red.'

The luxury European SUV that Finn took delivery of a couple of days later had been awarded 'Car of the Year' honours for good reason but it was the colour that Hazel approved of the most—a shimmering, metallic red. The dealership had thrown in a state-of-the-art baby car seat that Finn was currently carrying by its handle, with Ellie tucked up inside and clearly so comfortable she had fallen deeply asleep.

'I've decided it's time to road test this contraption,' he told Hazel. 'What are you and Ben up to?'

'We're watching Isabella. The farrier came again yesterday to do some more work on her hooves and…look… I think she's about to come out of the stables. But we've been here for fifteen minutes and she's just standing there watching us.'

Finn was watching Ben, who had slithered under the bottom rail of the fence and was now moving slowly towards Isabella.

'He's touching that toe down now.' He nodded. 'That's good.'

'It is.' But Hazel was frowning. 'I'm not sure it's good that he's in the paddock, though. I've heard donkeys don't like dogs much and I don't want him being chased. Hey… Ben… come here.'

Ben stopped, looked back at Hazel, wagged his tail but then lay down instead of coming back.

'Looks like he needs to think about that,' Finn said. 'I'll go and get him if Isabella doesn't like him. I was going to ask if I can borrow him, anyway.'

'What for?'

'To come into work with me and Beanie.'

'You're taking Beanie into work?'

'Sandra had to go and I have to film a *Call the Vet* episode—we're getting behind schedule. Anna and the others are only too happy to babysit while that's happening and Jude's keen on doing an update on Ben, with me giving him a check-up. I can talk about that X-ray you did the other day and pretend it was just done. The team love the footage of that emergency with Ben's accident and us working on him.'

'Oh...'

Hazel sounded as though she'd prefer to forget about her upcoming appearance on the show and that reminded Finn of why she might be reluctant. And then *that* reminded him not only of just how gorgeous he thought her body was but of that strange thought that hadn't been entirely suppressed. The one about wanting to have a future with Hazel? About her being the mother of children that he'd been so sure he'd never wanted to have? Wanting what they had together at the moment to turn into something he could trust to last for ever, even?

Oh, man...

Finn was confident that Hazel had no idea of what had just landed in his head again but maybe he needed to reassure her as well as himself that there was no pressure here. No expectations.

But then again, he really wanted her company.

Especially today. He'd made plans to try and make it happen, in fact.

'I got Sandra to make us a lovely picnic lunch before she left. Ham and egg sammies and some of that amazing caramel slice she makes.'

Hazel glanced down at the sleeping baby Finn was holding. 'But you're going into work now, aren't you? I don't need to be there until the afternoon clinic.'

'I thought I might be able to persuade you to come in a bit earlier,' he said. 'It's such a gorgeous day and we could have a picnic on the beach.' He offered Hazel his best smile. 'Jude says she's also keen to leave in the mention of your friend's refuge in the episode and follow that up soon so it would be good if you could talk to her about that.'

And that had been the reason she'd been brave enough to be on the show again, hadn't it? To help Two Tails. It might be too late because the last time she'd spoken to Kiara she'd said it sounded like her friend was starting to close things down at the refuge but it couldn't hurt to let people know how expensive it was to run places like Two Tails. If donations were raised, they could always be given to another animal refuge.

'Mmm...'

It was Hazel's unconvinced sound. And it made Finn stop trying to reassure either of them that there was no more than friendship involved here.

'I'd… I'd really appreciate your company, to be honest.'

It worked. She caught his gaze with the same kind of concern he'd seen in her eyes the night she'd agreed to help him when he was floundering so badly looking after Ellie. The kind of care he'd seen when she'd wanted to distract him from his awful day by introducing him to Isabella. The same kind of willingness to be as close as he wanted her to be that he'd seen in her eyes the first time he'd made love to her. A look that should be more than enough to make thoughts of a future with her even more compelling.

Hazel was frowning now. 'What's wrong, Finn?'

'The police think it's taking too long for Jamie to make contact. They think some publicity could help. That's the real reason I'm taking Beanie with me, today. I'm going to out myself as a grandparent later this afternoon and make a public appeal for Jamie to come forward.'

'Wow…' Hazel caught her lip between her teeth. 'That's going to be big news.'

'I'm not looking forward to the fallout,' Finn admitted. 'Right now I think I'm completely over being so well known. I'd rather be here with a baby and kittens and a limping dog and...' He shifted his gaze and a corner of his mouth lifted. 'And...that...'

Hazel turned her head swiftly to see what he was looking at. Isabella was walking towards them and she *wasn't* limping but she did pause to dip her head and sniff Ben, who lay very still and slowly wagged his tail.

'They're making friends,' Finn said quietly. 'How cool is that?'

Hazel smiled back at him. 'So cool...'

Oh... It was just as well that Finn was still holding the car seat or he might have swept Hazel into his arms to hold her as tightly as he could. To tell her just how important she was becoming to him.

To tell her that he loved her?

Not as in being in love with her, of course, because he had been burned too deeply to ever be capable of feeling like that again. But caring deeply about someone was love. Friendship was love, wasn't it?

'*We're* friends.' Finn tried to smile but his lips wouldn't quite co-operate.

'Mmm...'

Hazel had an odd expression on her face. One that he couldn't interpret but he managed to find at least a crooked smile. 'Friends do things like have picnics together, don't they?'

She was turning to watch Isabella, who

was on the move again, but Finn could see that her lips were tilting into a smile of her own.

'You know what?' Hazel didn't sound as if she was aware of any undercurrents to his invitation as she held out the carrot to let Isabella bite the end off.

'What?'

'I think a picnic sounds perfect.'

CHAPTER EIGHT

IT WAS, INDEED, a perfect picnic.

Not just because they could avoid getting sand in Sandra's delicious food by using one of the picnic tables on the grassy area beside the beach. Or that they found a space in the shade beneath a tree so they didn't have to worry about either a young baby or an elderly dog getting too warm in the bright sunshine. Or even that they were within walking distance of work so there was more time to enjoy everything. Like the cloudless sky and soft breeze of a gorgeous spring day, the shrieks of happy laughter from children playing on the grass, building sandcastles on the beach or paddling in the wash of gentle waves and the barking of dogs chasing frisbees or balls. Fortunately, Ben was content to lie underneath the picnic table in the hope of some crumbs falling so he wasn't in any danger of damaging his healing fracture. His hope wasn't misplaced, either. Did Finn really think she couldn't see him slipping tiny slivers of ham and cheese under the table?

And it was Finn who unbuckled Ellie from her car seat and lifted her when she finally woke up and started whimpering.

'Look at that, Beanie.' His hands circled the baby under her armpits as he held her up, turning her towards the beach. 'Can you see those big kids making sandcastles and going in the waves? We'll be able to do that soon, won't we?'

Ellie didn't appear to be impressed as her whimpering got louder. Ben crawled out from under the table to find out what was going on and Hazel put her hand on his head to reassure him that there was nothing to worry about.

Finn lifted the baby high above his head. 'Baby aeroplane…?' He swooped her gently from one side to the other.

She liked that more. The whimpering stopped but there was no hint of a smile yet. Still holding her securely between his hands, Finn dropped her to the same level as his face.

'*Boo*…' he said.

Ellie looked startled, her eyes comically wide. Then she opened her mouth and Hazel thought she was going to start wailing but, instead, her lips curved into the biggest grin ever and she began to make odd, hiccupping noises.

'Oh, my God…' Hazel said. 'I think she's laughing…'

Finn repeated the lift and drop and elicited another huge grin and the sound effects. This time, Ellie waved her arms up and down as well.

'She wants me to do it again,' Finn said. But, as he lifted the baby past his face, he frowned and then leaned closer to sniff her.

'Uh, oh…'

He hesitated for a split second and then he was grinning again as he changed direction and pushed Ellie towards Hazel instead of lifting her above his head.

'Isn't it your turn in the nappy roster?'

Hazel laughed. 'Uh-uh… Grandpa. It's definitely your turn.'

But she automatically reached out to take the baby and, for a moment, as they transferred her safely they were both holding her at the same time. Holding each other's gazes as well and they were both laughing and…

And it felt like one of *those* moments.

Pure love.

Not simply the love that Hazel had for this

man. It was love for the adorable Ellie as well. And for Ben, who had put a paw onto her knee to let her know he was close. For baby aeroplanes and first laughter and the whole background of sunshine and good food and other families enjoying themselves.

Other families…

Yes… Because that was what this felt like. A family of her own. A perfect family.

The final piece of a puzzle that had been coming together piece by piece, day by day as Hazel fell more and more in love with Finn. After what he'd said earlier today about preferring to be in his country property, in this fantasy they'd created of an idyllic home for children and pets, that seed of hope that had been growing—despite Hazel's determination to be realistic—suddenly sprouted leaves.

Not that Finn seemed to be feeling it, mind you. Hadn't he reminded her that they were simply friends, like they had witnessed Isabella and Ben becoming this morning? And, right now, it simply looked as if he was having fun. He was even laughing.

'Just kidding,' he said. 'But, if you could hold her for a sec, I'll go and get the nappy bag. I left it in the car. Or why don't we pack up and head into work now that we've had lunch? We can change her pants, heat up her bottle, hand her over to Anna and then we'll be all set to get on with the rest of the day.' He was already collecting the food containers to pack away leftovers. 'I know you don't need to start the clinic for a while but I'm sure Jude would love to have a chat with you before we get rolling. And, you could be there for Ben's examination, too, perhaps?'

Hazel shook her head. 'No. You can have all the on-camera limelight this time.' She cuddled Ellie closer. 'I'd rather deal with the dirty pants.'

This felt…normal.

Okay…a bit weird, maybe. Finn had just been outdoors in the warmth of the spring sunshine, seeing the sparkle of it on a gloriously blue sea, and here he was inside, with someone dusting powder on his face so that his skin wasn't going to be shiny under the lights as they filmed enough material to cover a couple of episodes of *Call the Vet* to catch up on scheduling deadlines.

Jude the producer was clearly thinking even further ahead, and she'd cornered Hazel as she was checking her list of patients booked in for the upcoming afternoon surgery hours.

'So…obviously we can't use all the footage of the surgery you did on the old stray dog but…wow…we all absolutely adore what you said about your mate's refuge. We'd call the episode "Two Tales" and find an example of a really heart-warming before and after story. Can you give me the contact details for…what was her name?'

'Kiara. Kiara Brail.' Hazel was sounding cautious, however. 'I don't think she's going to be interested in a television appearance for no good reason, though. She'd only let you in if it was going to benefit her refuge in some way and she's under so much financial pressure, she's on the point of closing.'

Jude flapped her hand. 'I'm sure we can rustle up a decent donation upfront.'

'Maybe I should talk to her about it first. She's got a lot on at the moment.'

This time, Jude shrugged. 'Up to her. And it would actually be better to wait so that we could use the dog that had the surgery. And you haven't found a proper, forever home for him yet, have you?'

'No. I'm lucky enough to be fostering him myself until he's recovered from the surgery.'

Finn shook his head to dislodge any loose particles of powder as the makeup technician turned back to her kit. He could see Ben waiting patiently with Anna in the consulting room where the camera crew were setting up and, when he shifted his gaze, he saw that Hazel had been looking in the same direction. Their gazes snagged for a heartbeat.

'And after that? Is he going to get the happy ending that would be exactly what all the fans of *Call the Vet* would want?'

'I don't know,' Hazel said quietly. 'But I certainly hope so.'

How amazing was it that you could read so much into a split second when you had eye contact with someone that you were getting to know really well? Finn knew how much Hazel loved Ben. Even though she'd never said anything, he also knew that it would be a dream come true for her to live somewhere she could keep Ben with her for the rest of his life. The determination to help her was born in that moment. Because, if anyone deserved to have a dream come true, it had to be Hazel.

'We'll keep in touch, then.' Jude was sounding less enthusiastic now. 'It is just an idea at this stage, of course. We've got lots of other exciting things on the boil for our Dr Finn.'

Yeah… Like sending him out to rescue a platypus or Tasmanian devil? Or making a fool of himself on a celebrity cooking show? Finn shook his head when the makeup technician turned back to him with a mascara wand in her hand.

'No, thanks,' he said firmly.

'Fair enough. Let's give your hair a comb and get a bit of hairspray on, at least. You look like you've been out surfing or something.'

'Nah…' Finn shoved his fingers through his hair. 'I'm going for the natural look today.'

The natural look? The kind of look that went with just hanging out with someone whose company you really enjoyed. On a beach. Or out in the countryside, watching a donkey walk freely, without severe pain, for possibly the first time in years. Knowing that a small black dog was getting pleasure from scraps of a picnic lunch he was thoroughly enjoying himself. When had he last had a picnic, for heaven's sake? Lunch with Shannon had usually been a freebie at some Michelin starred restaurant eager to court the approval of an influencer's hundreds of thousands of followers.

And what about how it felt to listen to a baby laugh for the very first time…?

Yeah…it was more than weird having

makeup thrown at you and knowing you'd be under the bright lights with cameras in your face for the next few hours. It felt fake. Irrelevant?

Except it wasn't really irrelevant, was it? Finn wanted the footage of Hazel operating on Ben to be used because he wanted people to see her skills and passion and her kindness, which were all things he loved about her. And he wanted the follow up episode to show Hazel and Ben living happily together—not in a basement flat—and so this bit that would be filmed today and used to link those 'two tales' was important, too.

'Ben came in as an emergency a bit over a week ago after being hit by a car and suffering a fracture of the tibia, which is the shin bone.' Finn had Ben on the table, a short time later, and he was stroking the dog's silky head. 'My amazing colleague, Dr Hazel Davidson, used specialised implants of a bone plate and screws to stabilise the broken bones. You can see them clearly on this X-ray that was taken recently.'

Finn picked Ben up and held him under his arm as he moved to the illuminated screen on the wall, knowing that the cameraman would be zooming in on the image.

'This smudgy bit here is the callus forming over the fracture line. A callus is a type of soft bone that replaces a blood clot where the bone is broken. It can hold bone together but isn't strong enough for the leg to be used but...' He smiled as he looked down at Ben, who very obligingly looked up and licked his neck. 'Ben's doing very well. In another couple of weeks, that fracture line will have disappeared completely and a month or so after that, we'll expect him to be running around just as good as new, chasing a ball, maybe.'

At least that point in Ben's recovery was far enough in the future to not have to think about it being the end of Hazel having a reason to live in his house.

With him...'?

It was still weeks away, Finn reminded himself, as they finished filming with Ben and set up a new case for Dr Finn to diagnose and treat. And he had far more important things to sort out before he let himself wonder how much he might be going to miss Hazel's company. Or whether Hazel might miss being with him? It wouldn't be a problem to sidestep thinking about it at all, actually, given how much practice he'd had doing exactly that. The easy way was to take emotion out of the equation by focusing on something practical. Like finding a place for

Hazel to live with Ben. Maybe not too far away from where he was living, so that they wouldn't lose the special friendship they'd discovered?

The simplest solution would be to help her find and buy a suitable property of her own but, if Hazel had that kind of money available, she would probably have done that for herself already and even Finn's healthy bank accounts would be noticeably dented by the kind of prices Sydney properties were going for these days. His Coogee Beach penthouse apartment, for example, would sell for millions. Did he really need to live between two properties? Imagine what he could do with that kind of money at his disposal?

It was precisely the kind of practical problem that Finn knew he could solve without his involvement threatening to become too emotional. And he would solve it. Later. There were other things that were a lot higher on his current list of priorities and the most important one was Beanie. They'd been in limbo, trying not to scare the baby's mother further into hiding, doing what they could to track her down discreetly while giving her the opportunity to make contact herself, but they had to accelerate the process somehow. Jamie had taken herself to a very isolated town in outback Australia to give birth. If she was already on the run again, the more time she had, the harder it would be to find her.

Fifteen-minute appointments were never quite enough but, today, the pressure was almost welcome because it kept Hazel's mind firmly on her job and not thinking about Finn being in front of the cameras in the adjoining consultation room. But, even that level of focus and the need to keep to time as much as possible wasn't quite enough to dispel that...what was it, exactly? A hollow sensation was the best way she could describe it. A bit like embryonic fear, perhaps.

Hazel knew it had been the picnic that had left this hollow sensation in its wake because she'd recognised the core of what family felt like, had felt an almost desperate longing to be able to make it the centre of her own life but was also aware that this particular combination might not last much longer. Because Finn hadn't noticed that feeling of family. Or maybe he had and it simply wasn't something he wanted in his life. And maybe the clock had started ticking in a countdown for his return to his normal life. He was not only filming a new episode of *Call the Vet*, he would be making another television appearance later to try and speed up the conclusion of the current disruption in his life that the arrival of his granddaughter had created.

One patient after another got called in from the waiting room for Hazel and it was a struggle to keep appointments anywhere near on time. She had to sedate a young beagle in order to extract a grass seed from his ear and the elderly, overweight Labrador was clearly showing the signs of diabetes and needed more than simply a blood test.

'Take this flat container,' Hazel told the owner, 'and take Penny over the road to that nice grassy area by the beach.'

Where she and Finn had had that gorgeous picnic that was already beginning to feel like a memory filed away in an album to be opened in years to come. Would she still remember the longing? And the hollow aftermath? Would it be a lovely memory because the dream had come true and they'd ended up being that family, or would it create heartache because the dream had evaporated?

Hazel shook the thought away. 'If she's urinating as frequently as you've told me, it shouldn't take too long to get a sample. Walk a little bit behind her and slide the container underneath when she squats. Just slowly—you don't want to give her a fright.'

'What do I do with it then?'

'We'll give you a jar, as well. You can tip the sample into that and bring it back. With both the urine and the blood sample we'll be able to make some decisions about how we start treating Penny.'

'It's bad, isn't it?' The dog's owner had tears in her eyes. 'If she does have diabetes? Can't it make you go blind?'

'Let's take it one step at a time. We're going to take good care of her and there's no point crossing bridges before we even know they're there.'

It was advice Hazel needed to take herself, she decided, as she led the way to the waiting area. One step at a time was all she could take because she had no idea what the next turn in her life might be or when it might happen. What she did know was that today's step belonged to Finn as he went public to try and make contact with his daughter and he needed her support. The timing of walking with Penny and her owner to the front door was spot on and she managed to catch Finn's gaze and offer an encouraging smile before joining other staff members who were standing to one side to watch.

He wasn't smiling as she watched him facing not one, but two sets of television cameras on the steps outside Coogee Beach Animal Hospital. Jude and her team were filming the news crew and the young reporter about to interview Finn. Because this was about the star of *Call the Vet* and they might want to include the footage in a later show?

Hazel's heart was sinking as she let her gaze settle on Finn's face. Was it the natural lighting that was making him look so much older and more serious or simply that he wasn't exuding the light-hearted, roguish charm that had made him such a celebrity? That the blanket-wrapped bundle in his arms wasn't a domestic pet of some kind was making a contribution to the atmosphere being so sombre, but what made it dramatic enough to have paused any normal services at this veterinary hospital was the fact that Finn was flanked by a uniformed police officer on one side and a motherly looking woman that had to be Margaret from Social Services on the other.

The young reporter was facing the cameras to one side of the trio to start with, a hand raised to gesture towards the big red letters above the hospital's entranceway.

'We're here today on the set of one of Australia's most popular television shows, *Call the Vet*, but it's not because of one of the an-

imals that the star of the show is caring for.'
The reporter turned towards Finn. 'It's about
a small baby who's been in the care of Dr
Finn because…?' He held the microphone
out, his words trailing off in an invitation
for Finn to explain for himself.

Hazel found herself holding her breath
as she watched Finn take a deep breath. He
was gathering his courage and she had to
stop herself walking towards him to stand
by his side and offer him some of her own.
He didn't look at the cameras as he spoke
but he looked down, at the face of the baby
sleeping in his arms.

'As unbelievable as it seems and, trust
me… I was as surprised as anyone to find
out—this beautiful little girl is my granddaughter.'

'Sorry…did you mean daughter?'

'No. She's my granddaughter.'

Hazel could see the way Finn took a deep
breath and she could hear the pride in his
voice. Wow…he'd come a long way from
the moment he'd been so alarmed by what
the title of grandfather might do to ruin his
image and lifestyle. She was so proud of him.
That seed of hope sent up another shoot as
well. He *did* feel the bond of family. And he
had wanted her here with him today.

'She was left in your waiting area over a week ago, yes?' the reporter stated. 'Abandoned.'

'She wasn't abandoned.' It was Margaret who spoke. 'She was left, for whatever reason, in the care of someone known to be a family member.'

The reporter nodded but instantly turned back to Finn. 'How can you be so sure that you're related to her?'

'There was a note with her that indicated a connection.' Finn looked up as he spoke. 'It was enough for me to take on the responsibility of caring for this baby—with the permission and support of both the police and Social Services—and to have DNA testing done. And that's why I can be very sure that I'm related to her. The test results were very clear. This little girl's mother is a daughter I never knew I had.'

There was a moment's silence then, as if everyone knew how shocking this news was going to be to a lot of people.

The reporter targeted the senior police officer next. 'What did the note say?'

'This is an ongoing investigation. We're not going to reveal information that might jeopardise that.'

Finn turned to look directly at the camera.

He looked in control now, Hazel thought. As comfortable as he was when he was filming his own show.

'You're not in any trouble, Jamie,' he said quietly. 'But we need to make sure you're okay. That we can provide any help you might need.' He paused and took another breath. 'Please come forward,' he added.

He was smiling at the camera now. A slow, totally genuine kind of smile. The kind that, even in these extraordinary circumstances, was enough to give Hazel that melting sensation deep inside. So were the soft words he finished with.

'I'd really like to meet you.'

Thanks to social media, nobody had to wait for an evening news bulletin to find out about breaking headlines and, while the startling news that Australia's most eligible bachelor was actually a grandfather wasn't exactly of international interest, it was certainly making a big splash locally.

As they made the journey back out to the Blue Mountains, Finn's phone was running hot with requests for appearances and interviews. By the time they got back to the house, clips of his interview were being shared and shared again.

'You did really well,' Hazel told him. 'I'm sure somebody's going to come forward.'

'Hmm…' Finn was shaking his head, looking at the screen of his phone as he waited while Hazel held the front door as Ben slowly climbed the steps to the veranda. 'Good grief…there are pictures here of me at university. How on earth has someone got hold of them so fast?'

'Have you any idea how many articles have been published about you in the past few years?' Hazel closed the door after Ben came inside. 'You'd only have to do an internet search to find hundreds of pictures.'

Finn led the way towards the kitchen. He put Ellie's car seat on the table and began to undo the safety harness buckles but he was looking at Hazel as he smiled wryly to acknowledge her point.

'Don't know about you,' he said, 'but I could use a glass of wine.'

'Sounds good,' Hazel agreed. 'It's been quite a day, hasn't it?'

'There's white in the fridge. Red in the wine rack in the pantry. Champagne in the cellar.'

Hazel opened the fridge. 'Good to know. We'll find it when it's time to celebrate.'

Finn lifted Ellie from the car seat. 'Yeah…

that's not yet, is it? Who knows who's going to come forward? What if it's not Jamie? What if it's Beanie's father and *his* family and they want to take her away?'

Hazel handed him a glass of wine. 'One step at a time,' she told him. 'That's not a bridge that's even on the map at the moment. Why don't we go and sit on the veranda for a few minutes and enjoy this wine and the sunset?'

Finn smiled. 'You're full of good ideas.'

'Here's another one. Leave your phone in here.'

'Okay...' But the ping of a new alert made him glance at the screen as he put it down. 'Oh, no...'

Hazel's heart skipped a beat. 'What?' She stepped close enough to see what he was looking at. 'Oh, my God...who took that? That was hours before the news broke.'

It was a picture of Finn. Holding Ellie up in the air to play 'baby aeroplane'. It was also a picture of Hazel, smiling up at him and even Ben was included, with his paw on Hazel's knee. It was a picture that perfectly captured that family moment that was going to stay with her for ever. And that made it so intimate that it seemed a violation to have it out there for the whole world to stare at.

'I'm so sorry,' Finn said quietly. 'I never meant for you to get splashed all over social media. I've got used to ignoring trolls but...' He put his phone face down on the table. 'Just don't look at anything for a few days, okay?'

Hazel was still reeling from the exposure that image represented when they went out to the veranda. Surely it was obvious by the way she was looking at Finn in that photograph that she was in love with him? If he couldn't see it, no doubt there'd be plenty of others happy to comment on it.

'This is just the start, isn't it?' she asked quietly. 'It's going to get worse.'

'Not tonight,' he said. 'Tonight it's just us.' He offered a gentle smile as he settled Ellie into the crook of his arm and then raised his glass. 'And, hey...it's a lovely photo. A real family picnic...'

Oh...that look in Finn's eyes. As if he really thought of them as a family. As if he wanted it to be real as much as Hazel did. It was a moment of teetering and it felt like Finn was about to say something that could make that happen. Except he didn't say anything because the sound of tyres crunching on gravel made them both turn their heads.

A police car was coming down the long

driveway towards the house. Ben barked as it stopped by the front door. Ellie began crying as two people got out of the back seat. The police officer that Hazel recognised from the interview this afternoon stayed in the car, along with a uniformed driver. One of the people that got out was Margaret. The other was a young girl with long dark hair, wearing a hoodie and ripped jeans.

Finn had gone very pale as he stood up. They both knew who this had to be but Margaret told them anyway.

'This is Jamie,' she said to Finn. 'Your daughter. Elena's mother.'

Again, Finn looked as though he was about to say something. Again, he didn't get the chance, because Jamie spoke first.

'I've come to get my baby back,' she said.

CHAPTER NINE

IT WAS A kick in the guts like no other.

Finn could only stand there and stare, the protective cover blown off that part of his heart where overwhelming emotions had been shut away. He took in the girl's tall, slender body, high cheekbones and the long hair that matched dark, dark eyes. That the look he was getting from those eyes was frankly hostile didn't make any difference and the words that finally emerged from his throat were as raw as the wound that had just been reopened.

'You look just like your mother…'

So like her that Finn could actually feel the memory of the piercing intensity of that first love in his life. The *only* love.

'How would you know?' Jamie's tone was a sneer. 'It's eighteen years since you even wanted to see her.'

'Let's go inside,' Margaret suggested. She

was looking past Finn. 'Maybe we could make some tea?'

She was talking to Hazel, of course, but the reminder that he wasn't alone made Finn turn his head. Ellie was still there in his mind, along with that memory, so it was impossible not to make a comparison and they were so, so different. The difference between a warm glow rather than a shower of fireworks. A softness rather than endlessly fascinating curves and angles.

A friend, not a lover.

But it was a friend that Finn badly needed right now. An anchor that he knew he could trust as soon as his gaze met hers. And it wasn't just that he'd always been able to rely on her support. Hazel had become an integral part of the huge change that was happening in his life—a change that had been settling into a new normal in the last few days but was suddenly being upended again. Maybe even Beanie was sensing a new disruption and that was why she was crying so much more loudly than usual.

'Let me take her.' Hazel was close enough to touch his arm. 'I can make her a bottle at the same time as the tea. Unless...' She looked at Jamie, who glared back at her, her lip curling, as she watched Hazel gather Ellie into her arms.

'That's a great idea.' Margaret spoke calmly but gave her head a tiny shake, as if to warn them not to expect Jamie to want to take responsibility for her baby too soon. 'We all need to have a chat, I think.'

'I just want my baby back,' Jamie muttered. She was still watching Hazel, Finn noticed. Sideways glances as she cuddled Beanie, her soft words to the baby still drowned by the unhappy cries.

'That's exactly what we need to have a chat about.' Margaret's tone was kind, but firm. 'You've been living on the streets, Jamie. We'll have to find a better place than that if you're going to look after little Elena, won't we?'

It seemed that Jamie wasn't ready to chat about anything, anytime soon. Ten minutes later, they were sitting at the kitchen table with mugs of tea in front of them but it was Margaret who was doing the talking.

'So Jamie saw you on television in a shop,' she explained to Finn. 'And she went into a nearby police station. That was where I was taken to meet her and we had a talk while I got her something to eat. She only agreed to come and see you if you weren't told she was coming.'

'But how did she know who I was in the first place?' Finn asked. 'Who even suggested that I was her father?'

'We talked about that, too.' Margaret nodded. She tilted her head, looking at Jamie, who was sitting with her hood up and head down, making her face invisible. 'Do you want to tell Finn about that, Jamie?'

There was no response but Finn saw a movement that suggested Jamie was still keeping a close eye on Hazel, who was sitting at the table with them, giving Ellie her bottle of milk. She did care about her baby, he thought. That gave them something in common, at least. Somewhere to start?

Margaret ignored the lack of response from the teenager. 'Jamie knew she had the opportunity to go to the Department of Child Protection to search for her biological family when she turned eighteen and, because she was pregnant with her own child, she decided she would do that. She…um…was ready to ask for support.'

'Money.' The word was a snap from Jamie. 'That's all I want from you. Lucky you're rich, eh?'

'I'll give you whatever support you need,' Finn said quietly.

'Yeah, right…' Jamie's snort was dismissive. 'Like you did for my mum when *she* got pregnant.'

'I didn't know about that. I had no idea you existed, Jamie…and…and I can't tell you how sorry I am. I'm prepared to do whatever I can to try and make up for that but…'

'But you didn't bother when it really mattered.' Jamie was on her feet. 'You didn't try and find my mum, did you? And she never stopped telling me how wonderful *you* were. How much she loved you…'

Oh…that hurt. Finn caught the flash of sympathy from Hazel. She knew it was true. She'd said that Ellie must have loved him to have called her daughter after him. That their love had been precious…

'Her father told me she'd got a job up north. That she'd had enough of school. Had enough of me…' Finn had to swallow past the lump in his throat. 'Why didn't she *tell* me?'

'Maybe because she didn't want to ruin your life—the way her father told her she'd ruined hers. She was supposed to go away and have an abortion. He told her to never come back if she didn't.'

Finn closed his eyes as he remembered the pain of assumed rejection. The way he'd chosen to stop believing in love at that point and to protect himself from it ever happening again. He'd made the biggest mistake of his life, hadn't he? And being barely more than a child himself wasn't enough of an excuse.

'But I don't understand,' he said slowly. 'Why didn't she make contact later? Why wasn't I told when she died and you went into care? Somebody must have known the truth…'

Jamie folded her arms and turned her back on Finn. She walked towards where Ben was in his basket near the pantry door and the little dog stood up and wagged his tail.

'Ellie's mother.' It was Margaret who supplied the information Finn wanted. 'She was approached to take Jamie in when her mum died and she said it was impossible because of her family circumstances. She said Jamie would be much better off with a different family. What she did do, a few years later, was to write a letter which was to be kept with Jamie's records and given to her if she ever chose to try and find out about her background. That's how she knows about why her mum had to leave home. And about how you ended up being the famous TV vet.'

Finn was watching Jamie as she crouched beside Ben to stroke him. 'It must have been hard for you to leave your baby in the waiting room like that,' he said quietly. 'I'm so glad you trusted that I would take care of her.'

Jamie shrugged. 'I didn't think you'd want her,' she said. 'Any more than you wanted me so there was no point asking you. I had to make sure you'd take notice.'

'I want her in my life more than anything,' Finn told her.

'Depends on how much it's worth to you.' Jamie sounded offhand. 'If it's not enough, I'll take her away and give her to someone else.'

He had to shift his gaze to look at Beanie, as if to reassure himself that she was still here. Hazel seemed to sense that that wasn't quite enough. The bottle was empty now and she handed the baby to Finn, who held her against his shoulder. He was rubbing her back as he turned to try and talk to Jamie again.

'I want you in my life as well, Jamie,' he said. 'To be Beanie's mum and for me to be your dad. Or try to be. I know I don't know anything much about being a dad. Or a grandpa, for that matter, but I'm willing to learn. Stay here with me. Let's get to know each other before any big decisions are made.'

Jamie said nothing. She was sitting beside Ben in his basket now, her hood pulled over her forehead. Ben put his nose on her lap.

'It sounds like a good way to start,' Margaret said. 'Or, I can find some emergency accommodation for you, Jamie. For you and Elena. In a motel in the city, probably, but I can help you get settled. We'll all work towards doing what's best for both of you. You *and* your baby.'

'We've got everything you could need, here.' It was the first time Hazel had spoken to Jamie and she was walking towards her as she spoke. She crouched down when she reached the basket. 'You'll be safe, I promise. How 'bout staying just for tonight and then we'll talk about it some more tomorrow? We only ever need to take one step at a time.' She was smiling as she leaned down to pat Ben's head, her hand touching Jamie's. 'He really likes you,' she said softly.

Jamie stopped patting Ben. 'He's got something wrong with his leg. It's gross.'

'It got broken,' Finn told her. 'He was hit by a car.'

Jamie stood up, flicking a glance back at Hazel. 'So she's your girlfriend now? When

I looked you up on the Internet it said your girlfriend was that model chick who goes around in bikinis all the time.'

'Hazel's my friend,' Finn said, ignoring the reference to Shannon because his love life was none of Jamie's business. None of anyone else's business, come to that. The difficulty in keeping personal things private was a real downside of being a celebrity. The anonymity of this time of hiding out in the country had been surprisingly enjoyable in more ways than he'd realised.

'Hazel's a vet, too,' he added, to take the conversation in a less personal direction. 'We work together. She was the one who did the surgery on Ben to fix his leg and she's staying here to help look after him. And to help me look after Beanie.'

He didn't look at Hazel as he spoke because it felt wrong, labelling her as simply a 'friend'. She was a lot more than that, wasn't she? But right now wasn't about Hazel. It wasn't about himself. It certainly wasn't about whatever new level he and Hazel had found in their relationship with each other or any possibilities the future might or might not hold. This was about a lost teenager who was a mirror image of a girl he'd loved so much, so long ago. And it was about a tiny baby who was ultimately vulnerable. A baby he had bonded with. A tiny person that he was not only responsible for—he had fallen in love with her.

Jamie looked up at him, her eyes narrowing. 'Her name's Elena, same as my mum. Why are you calling her a stupid name like "Beanie"?'

Everything had changed.

That moment, on the veranda, when Hazel had actually thought that Finn was about to say something that would somehow magically weld them into a family and give them a future, felt like a lifetime ago. A dream that she had been rudely awakened from by the stormy arrival of an unhappy teenaged mother.

The daughter Finn had never known existed but who apparently looked exactly like her mother—the love of his life. No wonder he was devoting all his time to try and connect with Jamie. Or that there was never a moment that it was just him and Hazel and Ellie in the kitchen or on the veranda. Having a glass of wine or supper in the evening or breakfast in the early morning and watching kangaroos on the far side of the paddocks near the trees that the sulphur-crested cockatoos loved to visit.

Hazel was doing her best to be encouraging and supportive but it was getting hard not to start feeling a bit superfluous. Sandra had been here more often to help with meals and housework and baby care, which was great because Jamie certainly wasn't showing any interest in anything other than sleeping, eating and shopping. Finn had taken her into the city on more than one occasion to buy clothes and toiletries and the kind of electronic accessories that all teenagers apparently couldn't live without, like the latest phone.

Margaret was a frequent visitor and Hazel knew that all options were being explored for Jamie and Ellie's futures, including formal adoption of them both by Finn. She'd heard snatches of conversations in the house.

'You could go back to school. Go to university if you wanted...'

'Why would I want to do that? You're rich enough. I don't need a job.'

'We could all live here. It would be a wonderful place for Beanie to grow up.'

'Out in the middle of nowhere? Are you freaking kidding?'

Jamie was hostile and Hazel could understand that. She'd been deprived of a father all her life. Deprived of a real family by the sound of it, as well, and she'd lost the freedom of a normal early adulthood by becoming a mother at such a young age. She could also understand why the focus had to be on Jamie but it was hard to maintain the sympathy as one day trickled into the next and the girl was still refusing to help care for her baby. She didn't want to feed her or bathe her or even pick her up for a cuddle and it seemed like Ellie was aware of the rejection because she was unsettled. She hadn't smiled, let alone laughed, since the day of their picnic.

While Finn was spending all his time at home, Hazel was spending more and more of her time at work. It was no problem to take Ben with her, Sandra was more than happy to take responsibility for Mittens and her kittens and it was a relief to be away from the tension in Finn's house. Even better to be kept so busy doing what she did best, with busy clinics and long theatre sessions. It was high time she spent a few hours at Two Tails, too, either helping in Kiara's veterinary clinic or in the refuge. She wanted to see for herself how well Bunji the dog was doing with her treatment and, well…she could do with a friend to talk through how this new twist in Finn's life crisis was affecting her.

She couldn't plan the visit until she'd got through the rest of the appointments for this afternoon's clinic, though. Penny the Labrador was next for a consultation to see how her owner was coping with having to administer insulin injections at home and whether the old dog's blood glucose levels were back within an acceptable range.

She opened the door and walked into the waiting area, looking forward to seeing Penny again, but she found her view of people sitting around the edges of the space was blocked by a man who was interrupting Kylie the receptionist as she began greeting a woman who was next in line at the counter.

'How can I help you?' Kylie asked.

'So that's the spot, then?' The man was loud. 'Where the kid was dumped?' He was pointing towards the display of dog toys. He raised a camera and there was a whirr of sound as he took multiple shots.

Hazel almost groaned aloud. She'd been deliberately staying away from the fallout on social media to Finn's news, but she knew there was a lot of gossip going on, with him getting slammed for abandoning a pregnant girlfriend and ignoring parental responsibilities for decades, rumours that his days as a celebrity were over and unkind memes about skipping the demands of fatherhood to go straight for membership of the rocking chair and slippers brigade.

Hazel signalled Penny's owner but turned to Kylie before she led the way back to her consulting room.

'Do you need any help?'

'Nah… I was just about to tell him to leave.'

The man stared at Hazel. 'Hey… I know you. You're the one who was with Dr Finn down on the beach the other day, aren't you? His girlfriend?'

'Hardly.' Hazel even managed a huff of laughter.

It was easy enough to sound as if the suggestion was ridiculous. Finn had said so himself the night Jamie had arrived, hadn't he? She was his friend. End of.

'You need to leave,' she told the stranger. 'Or we'll be calling the police.'

'No worries.' The man sounded almost amused. He was moving to the front doors, but Hazel could hear his camera whirring again as she bent to pat Penny.

'Come on, sweetheart,' she said to the dog. 'Let's get on with the important stuff, shall we?'

'Wait…' It was the woman still waiting to speak to Kylie who called out. 'I think it might be you I need to talk to.'

'Oh?' Hazel waved at the open door to the consulting room. 'Take Penny through,' she instructed the dog's owner. 'I'll be with you in just a minute.'

'I saw you in the paper, too,' the woman said. 'With the dog.'

Hazel felt a shiver of something she didn't like. She could guess what was coming.

'Is he yours?' the woman asked.

'I'm looking after him,' Hazel said. 'He got hit by a car a couple of weeks ago and needed some fairly major surgery on a broken leg. We were told he was a stray.'

The woman nodded. 'That would fit. He looks a lot like my dad's old dog, Max, who went missing about four weeks ago, after Dad had a fall and had to go into hospital. One of the neighbours tried to hold onto him when the ambulance was driving away but he slipped his collar and ran off. Dad's terribly upset about it all.'

'Of course…' Hazel had to fight the wash of something a lot deeper than merely disappointment. She knew that returning him to a loving family would be the best possible outcome for Ben. It wasn't as if she even had a suitable place to keep him after she left Finn's property. This woman's father had probably raised the old spaniel since he was a pup and loved him even more than Hazel did.

'Come with me,' she said. 'He's in a crate out back in our animal room. You can check to see if it is…um… Max.'

Isabella the donkey was on the far side of her paddock when Hazel drove in late that afternoon, but she spotted the vintage red van and had learned that treats were not far away. By the time Hazel parked in front of the house and lifted Ben down from the back of the van, Isabella was heading in her direction—at a trot.

Hazel was standing there with her mouth open when Finn came around the corner of the veranda with baby Ellie in a front pack. He immediately saw why she was so blown away.

'Wow…look at Isabella go. Doesn't look like her feet are bothering her much at all now.' He was smiling at Hazel. 'Feels good, doesn't it?'

'So good.' She smiled back. Baby Ellie,

who was facing outwards in the front pack, didn't join in the smiling but she waved her arms up and down and kicked her feet in what looked like shared approval and, for a heartbeat, it felt like it had before Jamie had arrived.

'Ben looks just as happy as we are.'

The small dog was right beside the fence, his paws on a rail as he lifted his nose. Isabella was leaning over the top rail, reaching down to touch that little black nose with her lip. The gentle greeting between the animals should have made Hazel's smile widen but, instead, it was fading rapidly. Nothing was quite like it had been before Jamie's arrival and things were still changing.

'His name's Max,' she told Finn.

'What?' Finn looked startled. 'But…'

But she'd named this dog after her childhood companion. The animal who'd provided his solid warmth and unconditional love in moments that had felt like despair and, while they hadn't really talked about it yet, Hazel knew that Finn would understand exactly what that had been like for her. She could hear the echo of his voice as he'd told her something she was quite sure he'd never told anyone else.

'I was the kid no one had ever wanted, or not for very long, anyway...'

She swallowed hard. 'His owner turned up at work today. Or rather, the owner's daughter. Her dad, Frank, had a fall and broke his hip a few weeks ago—over near Bondi Beach. The ambulance got called and the police turned up to break into the house for them and it was all pretty chaotic and Ben... I mean Max, got upset. A neighbour tried to catch him and tie him up but he slipped his collar and ran away.'

Hazel couldn't meet Finn's eyes. Maybe she didn't want to see the sympathy she knew she'd find because it would just confirm how much everything was changing. And yeah... she'd known that this was a bit of a fantasy living here like a perfect little family, but... she'd also wanted it to last a bit longer, because she'd always known it was going to hurt when it ended.

'So what's going to happen?' Finn asked quietly. 'Does Frank have someone in his family who'll be able to look after Ben? Or will he be able to himself when he recovers?'

Was it deliberate, not using his real name? Did Finn want to keep in touch with that fantasy as much as Hazel did?

'I'm not sure. His daughter can't take him

because her husband has asthma and is allergic to dogs and her father can't look after him because he's going to have to go into a rest home. I said I'd go and talk to him in the next few days. I'll take… Max to visit…' Hazel's voice trailed into silence. She didn't want to say it out loud, that she'd always known that her time with Ben wasn't going to last that long. That her time with Finn was going to be just as temporary…

Finn was silent as well. Which was why it was so startling to hear the peal of laughter coming from the direction of the house.

Hazel raised her eyebrows. 'Jamie sounds happier.'

Finn shook his head. 'She's been lying around all afternoon, glued to that phone. I wish I hadn't bought it for her. She still won't talk to me. She still won't have anything to do with Beanie, either. She says what's the point when she's going to have a new mother soon?'

There was another burst of laughter as Hazel headed inside to go and find a carrot for Isabella and this time, she could see where it was coming from. Jamie was lying on one of the cane couches on the veranda, holding her phone above her face. It was the words that followed the laughter that made

Hazel stop in her tracks, however. So fast that Finn and Ellie almost bumped into her. A singsong collection of words that Hazel had heard before.

'*Who ate all the pies?*'

The taunt that never got old, as long as you had a fat kid to throw it at. There was a part of Hazel that suddenly felt about ten years old again. A part that just wanted to run away and hide.

She heard Finn suck in his breath. 'What's that supposed to mean?' he demanded, his voice dangerously soft as he stepped towards where Jamie was lounging on her back, holding her phone close to her face.

'You're all over the Internet,' his daughter told him. 'And it's kind of funny. Look...' She held up her phone where the headline was clearly visible even to Hazel, who hadn't moved any closer.

One Girlfriend at a Time, Please, Dr Finn!

The picture beneath the headline had been taken today. One of that volley of shots Hazel had heard as she'd bent down to pat Penny the Labrador so it was her backside that filled most of the photo. Her huge bum in those baggy scrubs. And, in case that part of her anatomy wasn't instantly recognisable, whoever put the article together had unearthed a screenshot from the first time she'd appeared on *Call the Vet*, with Finn beside her. Hazel had time, before Finn grabbed the phone and switched it off, to see that a third photo was also there—one of Finn at some social event, looking gorgeously formal in black tie attire with the stunningly beautiful, unnaturally skinny Shannon clinging to his arm.

The ten-year-old part of Hazel had long since fled and a far more current version was spinning out. She could just imagine the thousands of comments that would be racking up below articles like this. The comparisons being made. The vicious bullying that keyboard warriors felt so entitled to unleash. At least she wasn't some vulnerable teenager. Hazel had heard it all before and she knew how to protect herself.

She'd broken the rules though, hadn't she? She'd let herself fall in love. Worse…she'd let herself start hoping.

Another thought surfaced, triggered by remembering that huff of laughter she'd produced when that man in the veterinary clinic this afternoon had recognised her as Finn's 'girlfriend'.

Hazel hadn't been surprised that the physical intimacy between herself and Finn had stopped after Jamie's arrival in the house because she understood that Finn's attention needed to be completely on trying to find a connection with Jamie and encouraging her to reconnect with her baby. But what if there was more to it, than that?

What if having someone else in the house had made him realise that a friendship with Hazel that was close enough to include sex would be acutely embarrassing if it became public? Had the sex only been a distraction from the boredom of being locked out of his normal, racy, celebrity lifestyle? Away from his gorgeous girlfriend, who might have dumped him but their separations never lasted that long, did they?

Everything wasn't just changing. It was falling apart. Imploding.

And, whatever direction Hazel's mind darted towards, she could only see it getting worse. The more she was seen with Finn, the more comparisons would be made. The more people would be laughing, as Jamie had been, at the very idea of her being his girlfriend. And, even if Finn didn't think that, he'd be influenced by it, wouldn't he? He'd admitted how angry he'd been when he thought he'd been rejected by Jamie's mother. How determined he'd been to become rich and famous so that he could be safe from that ever happening again.

Being mocked on social media would have been his worst nightmare not long ago and yes... Hazel could see he was angry now. His face was set in grim lines and Ellie must have picked up on the tension because her little face was crumpling and the whimpers were starting.

'I'm keeping this phone,' he snapped at Jamie. 'And you can apologise to Hazel.'

'What for?' Jamie sat up but avoided making eye contact with Hazel. 'It's not me calling her fat, is it? And you said she wasn't even your girlfriend.' Then she shrugged. 'But, hey...if I'm in the way of you two hooking up or something, I can always go somewhere else. And take my kid.'

Finn stepped closer to Jamie and it was obvious he was struggling to keep control of what he was about to say to his daughter. Ellie started crying. Loudly. Ben was slinking into the house, his tail between his legs, and Hazel realised that, actually, what was going on here had nothing to do with her. She was just muddying the waters of something

far more important that needed to be sorted
out and her heart was sinking like a stone.

Maybe Jamie was jealous of the easy
friendship that she and Finn had. Or perhaps she suspected there'd been something
more going on. Whatever... Hazel could well
be unintentionally blocking the attention that
Jamie was actually desperate to receive from
her father. And if Finn confronted Jamie over
finding hurtful comments about her amusing, any hope of a positive relationship developing between them might be pushed even
further away.

Hazel had to try and do something to de-
fuse this situation. Fast—before anything
more damaging was said. It was possibly
the last thing she *could* do to help Finn get
through this life crisis and, while her heart
was breaking, she still wanted to do whatever she could to support him.

'I didn't tell you,' she said into the simmer-
ing silence, her voice artificially bright. 'But
my friend Kiara up at the Two Tails refuge is
desperate for me to go and look after things
for a week or so while she's away. I can take
Ben with me. I know Sandra will be happy
to look after Mittens because she's offered
to adopt her if no relatives or friends of the
owner come forward. And Isabella will be

fine here by herself for now.' She turned to follow the little dog. She should just bite the bullet and start calling him Max, she thought, as she surrendered to the fragments of any fantasy evaporating. 'I just came home to pick up the things I'll need.'

Finn followed her inside.

'Please don't go, Hazel,' he said. 'I need you.'

It was far from the first time he'd said that to her. It was precisely what had pulled her in and started what had become such an irresistible fantasy. Had started the hope that she might mean something to him one day. Something that was strong enough to make her believe the impossible. And she had... briefly. Before the outside world had reminded her of why she'd never let herself truly believe.

'No, Finn,' she told him gently. 'You don't need me. You need to believe that you can get through to Jamie. That you can make this work. That's your *family* out there...'

He was shaking his head, rocking the still crying baby in his arms. 'She hates me. She doesn't believe that I didn't just abandon her.'

'I think she's pushing you away just because she's afraid of being rejected herself. Talk to her. Properly. Tell her what you told me about what it was like for you. She'll know how much you loved her mum. I knew…'

She knew that Ellie had been the love of his life.

How on earth had Hazel started to believe that Finn might love *her* that much as well? Even now, as she let herself sink into the way he was looking at her, she could still believe…

'Trust me,' she whispered. 'It will be better for everybody if I'm not here.'

Including herself?

Hazel paused only to dial Kiara's number before she drove away a short time later. Her friend must be busy out in the pens, she decided, as the call went to voicemail, but maybe she'd get the message before Hazel actually arrived at Two Tails.

'I'm heading your way,' she said. 'I'll fill you in when I get there but it's best if I get away from here and I need to go somewhere I can take Ben. I don't know if that job opportunity's still there—the one with that guy who needs you to live in and get a rehome settled?' Hazel started the engine of her van. 'But, if it is, this might be the ideal time to take advantage of it. I'm more than happy to take care of Two Tails for a week or so.'

She couldn't look back as she drove away because, if she saw Finn standing on the veranda, she might not hold onto the strength to do what she knew she had to do. Removing herself from this situation *was* going to be better for everyone.

Especially herself...

CHAPTER TEN

THERE WERE TEARS.

Of course there were. The staff at Frank's rest home were only too happy to welcome Hazel and Ben when she went to visit and there were very few dry eyes when the little black spaniel's entire body was wriggling with the joy of being reunited with his person, Frank, who was in a big, squashy reclining chair in the rest home's conservatory as Ben climbed up to snuggle in beside him.

The tears were too close to the surface anyway, for Hazel—they had been ever since she'd left Finn's house, so it was almost a relief to have a perfectly acceptable excuse to let some of them escape. She was quite well aware that the many tears that had been shed in the last days, due to heartbreak because a fantasy bubble had burst, were a kind of self-indulgence, really. After all, she'd always known that living her dream was only going to be temporary.

Maybe it hadn't been the best idea to take a week's leave from work to look after Two Tails because it had shut her off from the rest of the world and given her rather too much thinking time. She had a couple of hours in the afternoons of keeping surgery hours in Kiara's small vet clinic and Maureen, who'd been a friend of Kiara's grandmother, helped out in the mornings but, apart from that, Hazel was entirely alone with Ben and the handful of dogs left in the refuge now that it was being wound down.

In other ways, however, it helped quite a lot that Hazel had shut herself away. She only switched on her phone to make an occasional call and check messages, which kept her well away from the danger of tapping into whatever unpleasantness was still happening on social media. She would have loved to find out how things were going between Finn and Jamie but, instinctively, she knew that completely disappearing from Finn's life might convince Jamie that there were no barriers between her and her father.

In order to distract herself, Hazel was keeping herself as busy as possible. The pens for the dogs were probably being scrubbed twice as often as necessary, she had reorganised all the storage cupboards in the clinic and the dogs were all being very well exercised, apart from Ben, who still needed care even though he was almost walking without any limp at all now. In the evenings, with Ben asleep in his basket, Hazel still kept herself busy. Kiara's grandmother had been an avid collector of all sorts of things like lamps and ornaments and china and Hazel still had some work to do to meet the challenge of making sure they were all free from dust before Kiara came home.

Taking Ben to visit his owner in the rest home was another distraction and, although it happened days later than Hazel had promised Frank's daughter, it was the first foray away from what had provided a refuge for herself as much as the remaining residents.

So that made the tears feel excusable. It was probably also the reason that it had been so welcome to have someone to really talk to, after she and Frank and Ben had been left alone in the conservatory.

'Sorry... I've got to stop calling him Ben,' Hazel said, nearly an hour later. 'He's Max. And I think he's the happiest dog in the world right now.' She blinked hard, to prevent new tears trying to collect at the back of her eyes.

She could feel the joy in the connection between this elderly man and his old dog and the glow of that love reminded her of those special moments she'd had with Finn and Ellie—like when the baby had smiled for the first time. When they'd heard her laugh. When Finn had said that he really wanted to make love to her...

Oh, man... Missing someone was a kind of grief that could be astonishingly painful.

'You called him Ben for the best of reasons,' Frank said. 'I'm so glad you told me about your old dog. And about Two Tails and your friend Kiara. And Isabella the donkey.' He was smiling. 'And let's not forget the baby that arrived in your life on the same day that Max did.'

They'd been talking non-stop since staff members and other residents had left the three of them to enjoy the sunny corner of the conservatory uninterrupted. Or, rather, Hazel had been talking non-stop.

'Oh, help... I've been talking far too much. I've probably tired you out completely. Look, Max is so bored he's sound asleep.'

'Quite the opposite. I feel better than I have ever since the accident,' Frank said. 'Like I'm part of the adventure you're having. I hope you'll come back soon and give me an update.'

Oh… Hazel desperately wanted an update herself. But the longing to know how things were going between Finn and his daughter, whether Jamie had taken any step closer to bonding with *her* daughter or even how the kittens were doing was strong enough to be a warning that she was too involved already. It wasn't simply that she had cleared the way for Finn and Jamie to connect. Keeping up her own connection with them would only prolong the painful journey of getting back to her own real life.

'It's certainly been a roller coaster,' she admitted. 'And I've been short of people to talk to about what's going on in my life. No one that talks back to me, anyway.' She leaned over to stroke Ben. 'This little guy's a great listener, though.'

The dog didn't open his eyes but his tail thumped against Frank's legs as he felt Hazel's touch.

'He loves you,' Frank said quietly. 'And, you know what? I reckon you should keep calling him Ben because he doesn't care what he's called. He just wants to be loved by you.' He touched her hand. 'And I can see why he does. You're a very special person, Hazel Davidson. I hope you know that.'

Okay…blinking wasn't quite going to do the job with those tears. Hazel had to swipe away one that escaped. The words were a balm to a self-esteem that had been far too easily knocked back all over again, after reading what was being said about her, thanks to all those years of being bullied.

Finn had thought she was special, too, hadn't he? Hazel only had to remember the way he'd looked at her sometimes and, dear Lord, the way he'd touched her, to know that she hadn't been wrong to believe that was genuine. What she shouldn't have started believing in was that it could be her future.

He'd said it himself. That he'd been so devastated when the girl he'd loved had vanished from his life that he was never going to let anybody hurt him that much again and it was easy to translate that into him never letting himself fall in love again. Or trust in a future with someone. That was the real obstacle between Finn and his daughter connecting, wasn't it? They both needed to lower their barriers. To make themselves vulnerable. They both knew how much it hurt to lose someone they loved but…even the way

Hazel was feeling right now, she knew it was worth it.

'Did you really mean what you said about adopting Ben?' Frank had kindly busied himself scratching the dog's silky ears as Hazel found a tissue and got rid of those tears. 'Because, if you did, I would love you to do that. I can't think of a better home he could possibly have. Or a better name when it belonged to another dog you loved so much.'

'Of course I meant it.' Hazel nodded. 'Not that I actually have a suitable home just yet. I'll have to find somewhere new to live.'

'I was thinking in terms of "home" being more about people than places,' Frank said softly.

Hazel didn't want to let his words sink in. How sad would it be if she'd left more than simply Finn's property? If she'd walked away from the only 'home' she might ever find? No, she couldn't afford to think that.

'I've started looking already,' she assured Frank. 'I've got the rest of this week at the refuge—probably longer if I need it.'

'There's my house in Bondi,' Frank said. 'It'll have to get sold eventually, I expect, but you'd be welcome to live there in the meantime if it helps. That way, you'd be close enough to come and visit sometimes.'

'I'll do that anyway. *We'll* do that…won't we, Ben?' Hazel smiled as she got to her feet. 'Look at how much he's loving being here. It makes me think he might like to do visiting like this on a regular basis—for other people, as well, perhaps.'

'He's always loved people. And who wouldn't want cuddles like this? You know, that could be a way to get people interested in helping the refuge. It might even help solve those financial problems.'

'Something to think about, that's for sure.' Hazel got to her feet. 'Come on, Ben. We'd better get back to Two Tails and get to work. Those pens won't clean themselves and there's exercise and training that needs to happen.'

'Thank you so much for coming to me.' It was Frank's turn to dab at his eyes. 'I can't tell you how happy it's made me.'

'It's been such a pleasure,' Hazel said. 'And I should be the one thanking you. That kind of happy is contagious and it was exactly what I needed today.'

As always, the drive back to the Blue Mountains was another form of therapy for Hazel and, for the first time since she'd walked away from Finn, she was feeling hopeful again, which was probably due to

Frank's pleasure in her visit—and the nice things he'd said about her. He'd inspired her to not give up on the future of Two Tails and Kiara's vet clinic, either, and that positivity was growing to include what might be ahead for Finn's relationship with his daughter and his granddaughter. About a future that was grounded in family and was *real*—with all the highs and lows that real life delivered.

Their friendship was also real, she knew that. And friends didn't abandon each other when times were tough. Okay, she might be right in keeping out of the way for the moment, but that didn't mean she couldn't let Finn know that she was thinking about him, did it? That she cared...?

She turned her phone on as soon as she arrived back at Two Tails and texted.

Thinking of you. Hope it's all going well. xx

Finn hadn't realised he'd been holding his breath until the bleep of an incoming text message made him release it in an enormous sigh.

He'd come outside, after Beanie had finally exhausted herself enough by crying to fall asleep, because he had to try and ease the sheer frustration that was building to breaking point. In what was becoming an automatic habit, he'd picked up a carrot for Isabella on his way outside. He'd been waiting for the little donkey to trot over to the gate, his phone bleeped and when he looked at the screen to discover that it was Hazel messaging him he felt that tightness in his chest being released with that huge sigh.

To his surprise, it felt like something else was also being let go. Self-control, perhaps? The ability to convince himself that it was better for both of them that Hazel had left? Better for all of them, because if Jamie had gone any further down the track of enjoying the comments of those vicious online trolls that thought Hazel was fair game, he might have given up on ever connecting with this young woman who was his daughter and simply told her to get out of his life?

Surely that prickle behind his eyes and the new lump in his throat wasn't the threat of tears?

No...of course it wasn't.

It was just that things weren't going well at all, really, and knowing that Hazel was thinking about him was like...like feeling her touch.

He was just *missing* her, dammit...

'Nothing's been the same since our Hazel

left, has it, Isabella?' Finn hung onto the end of the carrot as the donkey gently took the pointy end between her teeth and then tilted her head sideways to break it off. 'No…that's not true, is it? Nothing's been the same since Jamie turned up.'

Maybe that should be since Beanie turned up. His life had been tipped upside down in an instant at that point. It had been Hazel who'd suggested the appalling possibility that the baby might be his granddaughter and what had his first thought been? That it would destroy his image. His television career. Possibly his entire lifestyle.

And what had Hazel said? That it could be the best thing that had ever happened to him. He'd started to believe that, too. How good had it felt that morning in the kitchen when Ellie had smiled at him for the first time? And when they'd both heard her first laughter on that picnic. And, if it hadn't been for Ellie—and Ben—it might never have occurred to him to spend so much time with Hazel and, quite apart from now having an infant in his life who'd totally captured his heart, getting so close to Hazel was competing for the status of being the very best thing that had ever happened to him.

'You miss her too, don't you, Bella?' Finn

gave the donkey the rest of the carrot and scratched her neck just behind her ear as she ate it.

Finn had such a clear image in his head of Hazel sitting on the veranda that first morning. In her PJs with all that gorgeous softness undisguised. He found himself smiling as he remembered the look of delight in her eyes when she'd spotted the kangaroos but then his smile faded as he remembered the look in her eyes when she'd told him that making love with him was the only thing she wanted…

That was what he was missing most of all. Not just the sex—although he had to admit his bed had never felt quite this lonely—but that closeness that came when he could sleep with her in his arms. A closeness that was there by just breathing the same air, actually. Hazel Davidson was the first person who had seen right through the image he'd created with his celebrity lifestyle and all the flashy tokens of his wealth and deemed them shallow. She'd recognised the unhappy, unwanted kid he'd been and she knew that so much of him now had been carefully crafted and…yeah…*fake*, but she still thought he was worth loving. Just by being there, Hazel could make this huge house feel like a home.

She'd created a glue that had made them feel like…a family.

And, despite having told Hazel that he didn't do dependants on a long-term basis, he desperately wanted that feeling back again.

But she'd gone—because she'd wanted to—and that feeling had gone, too. Over the last week, things had gone from bad to worse. Finn had tried to talk to Jamie, on several occasions, as Hazel had advised him to do. He wanted to succeed. To fix things. Not only to make up for not having been there for his daughter or even to stop history repeating itself with Ellie, but to honour the memory of Jamie's mother and her importance in his own story and…and he wanted Hazel to truly believe that there was nothing fake about him any longer. Maybe he even wanted her to be proud of him?

He knew Hazel had been right in thinking that being here alone with Jamie was his best, possibly only, chance to establish a relationship with the daughter he'd never known he had and he'd done his best to get her to believe that things would have been very different if he'd known about her existence but Jamie was still refusing to listen. She simply put her ear plugs in and watched videos on her phone or walked off and shut herself away in her bedroom.

It was getting harder to resist the urge to contact Hazel and ask for more advice but he'd already asked enough of her. Too much, perhaps. Was that part of the reason why she'd left? Did she need some space? If he had some good news to tell her, it would be a great excuse to make contact, but day after day was passing without any kind of breakthrough and now Finn was in need of some space himself. It was tempting to rely more and more on Sandra's help so that he could escape by spending more time at work in the city but his loyal housekeeper had finally lost patience earlier today, when Jamie had gone off to slam doors after Finn suggested she gave Ellie her lunchtime bottle.

'She needs her mum,' Finn had pleaded with Jamie. 'Please…just try?'

'I'm not going to *be* her mum. Who are you to try and make me, anyway? You didn't even *try* to be my dad. *You* never fed me, did you?'

The door slamming had made Ellie howl so much that Finn couldn't get her to settle, let alone drink her milk, and he was quite sure that she'd never been this grizzly or miserable when Hazel had been here to help. She was still crying and hungry when he'd rung work to let them know he couldn't come in this afternoon, after all. Sandra had apparently just remembered an appointment she couldn't break.

'Jamie needs boundaries,' Sandra had told Finn as she left. 'I know she's had a lot to deal with in her life but you've been tiptoeing around her and she's still behaving like a spoilt brat. My two cents' worth is that she needs you to be a parent and provide boundaries. You can't trust something if you don't have any idea what shape it is. What picture it's making.'

So here he was—outside, soaking in a moment of peace with a small donkey. The shape of a donkey's ear was an amazing thing, Finn thought, as he ran it through his hand. Isabella pushed her nose forward to lean her chin on his shoulder as he stroked her ear again and it made Finn smile. It also gave him a new thought. Maybe the good news to share with Hazel didn't have to be about his relationship with Jamie?

How happy would she be to know that this little donkey she'd rescued was enjoying being here this much? How much would she love to see it for herself? Was she busy at the moment? Two Tails refuge wasn't that far away, if she wanted to pop over for a cup of coffee or something. He wouldn't put any pressure on her to come back. Why would she want to, when Jamie had been so rude to her?

Finn picked up his phone again, to respond to her text message and invite her to come and visit, but he couldn't find the words he needed because there were others trying to come out.

I need you...

I miss you...

I miss that feeling of family we made together. You and me and Beanie and Ben.

There was something else that he needed to say even more urgently but he had no idea what it was with so many other words competing for his head space and then that effort was interrupted as the handset clipped to his belt crackled into life with the sound of a baby waking up and beginning to whimper. He stayed where he was for a long moment, however, trying to recapture the threads of what he'd been searching for, but the cries were getting rapidly more demanding and, to be honest, it was kind of a relief to be able to push it all to one side. Finn slipped his phone into his pocket without having responded to

Hazel's message at all and turned to go back to the house.

Then he heard another sound on the monitor. Jamie's voice.

'Fine… I guess I'll *have* to do something with you, then, if nobody else is going to.'

Finn could hear the sound of footsteps and the change in Beanie's cry as she was picked up. He increased his pace, as the sound of the baby crying got fainter with her being carried away from the baby monitor. Where was Jamie taking her? And what was she planning to do with her baby? Fear was competing with what felt like a certainty that Jamie would never harm Beanie but the need to protect his granddaughter was strong enough to override anything.

He paused in the wide hallway of the house when he was able to hear Beanie crying again. The sound was coming from the kitchen and it covered the sound of his footsteps on the polished wooden floorboards as he headed towards that part of the house. He slowed and then stopped just outside the door, to take a breath and not rush in looking like he thought he had to rescue the baby from a mother who couldn't be trusted, and that was when he heard the beep of the microwave as it finished heating something and the baby's cry changed to a hungry squeak. He stayed where he was for a moment longer.

'I told you I'd come back,' he heard Jamie whisper. A chair scraped on the floorboards. 'I told you that we'd be okay...'

She couldn't see Finn as he moved just enough to see past the open door. Jamie was sitting at the table, holding Ellie, whose face was bright red from her distressed crying. She slipped the teat of the bottle into the baby's mouth in what looked like a well-practised move and then sat very still, looking down at her baby.

Finn eased back before he was spotted. Beanie was clearly perfectly safe and the worst thing he could do right now might be to interrupt this moment of bonding that was finally happening again between a young mother and her baby. He could go back outside and talk to Isabella again but the temptation to return and try and build on Jamie's change of heart—to see if *he* could also find a connection between himself and his daughter—was getting stronger by the second.

When his gaze caught the spot under the tree where he'd parked his new SUV, he had a much better idea. He could take himself right away. Just long enough for that bond between Jamie and Ellie to take shape again.

Thirty minutes should do it, he thought. And that was more than long enough to drive over to Two Tails, which might solve the dilemma of what to say in a text message to Hazel.

If he could see her, surely he'd know what it was he wanted to say to her—whatever it was that he couldn't put in a text message.

He needed be close enough to touch her because missing her was a physical ache and nothing felt like it was in its right place. His life had been tipped upside down and shaken and there were pieces all over the place and there was only one way to deal with any kind of jigsaw. You had to pick up the first piece and make a start.

The easiest way to do that was to find the edge pieces, wasn't it? To make boundaries, as Sandra had suggested were needed. There was, hopefully, the shape of a new picture forming between Jamie and Ellie right now. Finn needed one that might make sense of what was happening to his life. And he needed a shape for what he and Hazel had found with each other because it didn't seem to have any edges at all and that was confusing. Because it couldn't be trusted?

Finn was ready to put his foot down as soon as he got to the road at the end of his long driveway. He knew where Birralong was and it wouldn't be hard to find the only animal refuge nearby. He waited impatiently for the automatic gates to slide open but he didn't put his foot down on the accelerator, after all. His car wasn't about to go anywhere. Because he could see another vehicle coming down the road. A vintage, red van that could only belong to one person.

Hazel turned in through the gates and stopped the old van alongside his shiny new SUV. Her driver's side window was only inches away from his. She was winding a handle to lower her window. Finn just needed to press a button.

'I thought I'd pop in,' Hazel said. 'You... you didn't answer my text.'

'I couldn't,' Finn said quietly. 'There were too many things I wanted to say so... I thought I'd come and see you.'

Hazel was holding his gaze. Because she wanted to, or because he had no intention of letting hers go? Maybe it didn't matter when he was looking at a reflection of what had to be showing in his own eyes. The sheer *relief* of being close again. The feeling that he'd not only found the first piece of that puzzle, it was the most important piece of all.

He wanted to reach out and touch her. No...what Finn actually wanted to do was to get out of his car. To reach in through Hazel's open window to hold her face gently between his hands and then lean in to kiss her absolutely senseless. Even the thought of doing that was tilting his lips towards a smile. And perhaps Hazel could read his mind because she was touching her bottom lip with the tip of her tongue.

That did it. Finn went to open his door but the vehicles were too close. And something else was creating static in the spell that had been cast the moment his gaze had captured Hazel's. She was aware of it as well and a frown was creasing her forehead.

'Is that Ellie crying?'

Finn killed the engine of his car. He hadn't realised that he still had the handset of the baby monitor clipped to his belt. Or that the range of the device extended this far. Jamie must have taken Beanie back to her bassinette after feeding her because she was obviously close to the monitor. He was frowning now, too. He'd never heard Beanie cry with this odd, high-pitched note in her voice.

And then the crying stopped abruptly and they could hear Jamie's voice.

'Oh, my God…what are you doing? What's happening…?'

There was the sound of rapid footsteps and

then a piercing shriek, but it wasn't coming from a baby.

'*Finn*…where are you? Something's wrong with Ellie. Something *bad*.'

Again, Finn could see exactly how he was feeling himself reflected in Hazel's eyes. He could see pure fear. He restarted the engine and began backing up so that he could turn the vehicle in front of the little red van.

'Follow me,' he called to Hazel. It was a plea rather than an instruction.

This time he did put his foot down but it still didn't seem fast enough. The voice he could hear was fainter now. Was that because of the engine noise or was Jamie getting further away from the monitor as she searched for him.

'*Finn*… Where are you?'

He could hear a choked sob.

'*Dad*…please… I really *need* you…'

CHAPTER ELEVEN

HAZEL HAD SEEN Finn shocked, as he had been when she'd suggested he could be the grandfather of the baby left in Coogee Beach Animal Hospital's waiting area. She'd been so disappointed at that point in time, not only because it made Finn seem so shallow but she'd been disappointed in herself at the same time. Because, even then, she knew she was in love with this man and how could her instincts have been so misplaced?

She'd seen him overwhelmed—lost, even—as he had been when she'd arrived that first evening in response to his plea for assistance in looking after that baby and when she'd seen the glimmer of potential tears in his eyes, she'd known that her instincts hadn't been so wrong, after all.

And when he'd spoken… *'I'm hopeless at this…'*

Oh, my…looking back, that was quite possibly the moment the love she'd had for Finn hidden in a secret place in her heart had broken out of any restraints. She had felt it like something melting. Trickling through her whole body.

And Hazel had seen him still devastated enough by what had happened so long ago to really shed tears and that had been the night she had given herself to him—body and soul—for as long as it could last.

But, right now, she was seeing something that took her love for this man to the next level. He was showing a determination to protect and care for someone he loved that was second to none. And, while this was directed towards his tiny, vulnerable granddaughter, that seed of hope that he could feel the same way about her had not been buried. Or, if it had, it was pushing its way clear with astonishing power. The way Finn had been looking at her just a minute or two ago, when they'd met at the end of the driveway. He'd been coming to see her. He had things he wanted to tell her and Hazel thought she might know what those things were because she had a few of her own things to say but, oddly, it felt as though they'd already *been* said. Just not aloud.

And, saying them aloud didn't matter.

Even thinking about them was no more than a background to what was going on in Hazel's mind as she watched Finn take charge of this emergency. Her thoughts were not even that coherent. She was aware of total confidence in his ability. Pride. A need to be by his side so that she could offer total support in whatever way she could.

'She's burning up,' Finn said, his hand gently covering Ellie's head. 'We need to bring her temperature down and then get her to hospital asap.'

'But what's wrong with her?' Jamie had both arms wrapped tightly around her own body but she was still shaking. 'What did I do wrong?'

'This isn't your fault,' Finn told her. 'It's quite likely that she's picked up some kind of infection. A high temperature can make a baby have a seizure, which is what was happening when you saw her body jerking.' He was peeling off the cardigan and booties that Ellie was wearing over her stretchy onesie. 'I should have realised she was off colour. She's been a bit grizzly all day.'

The baby was still grizzling now. An unbearably miserable sound.

'It's my fault,' Jamie insisted. Then she burst into tears. 'I miss my *mum…*'

Oh…there was so much more than merely acknowledging the absence of someone beloved in that cry. There was the echo of so much grief and lost opportunities and possibly the aftermath of feeling totally abandoned? It melted Hazel's heart instantly and it wiped the slate clean of any unpleasant behaviour or words that had come from Jamie up till now because she could understand exactly where it had come from. Hazel put her arm around Finn's daughter's shoulders.

'Of course you do, love. But you've got Finn here and…and that's a good thing, believe me.'

'He's just a vet,' Jamie sobbed. 'Ellie's not an animal.'

'He's your dad,' Hazel said quietly. 'And he's Ellie's grandad and he's going to take care of you both. He knows what he's doing.' She tried to give Jamie a gentle, reassuring squeeze. 'I'd trust him to look after me more than anyone else on earth.'

Baby Ellie was wearing only her nappy now. 'I need tepid water,' Finn said. 'And a sponge or a cloth. Could you get that, please, Jamie? In a bowl from the kitchen?'

'What's tepid?'

'Lukewarm. Body temperature.'

Jamie nodded, pulling away from Hazel's

arm to run from the room. It was only then that Finn caught her gaze and she could see the fear was still there.

'It's not impossible but I think Beanie's a bit young to have had a febrile seizure.'

'What else could it be?'

'If she didn't have an obvious fever, I'd be worried about a birth injury or a brain abscess or head injury.'

'And with the fever?'

Finn picked Ellie up and held her. She squirmed in his arms, still crying. 'The most worrying thing it could be is meningitis.'

'Do you want me to call an ambulance?'

Finn shook his head. 'The seizure's stopped and there's no sign of a rash. We'll take a few minutes to cool her down and then we'll drive her to the closest hospital ourselves. We'll be there before an ambulance could even get here.'

Jamie was back with a bowl of water and a kitchen sponge.

'Good girl.' Finn smiled at his daughter. 'Come over here. We'll put Beanie on her change table and you can sponge her down.' He turned to Hazel. 'Can you see if there was any liquid paracetamol in that box of pharmacy supplies? It might help to bring her temperature down.'

'Do you know where the box is?'

'I think Sandra tucked it away in the pantry. It got delivered in the first day or two after we brought Beanie home, remember?'

As if Hazel was ever going to forget. Especially that first morning when she'd woken up to find herself smack bang in the middle of a fairy tale. Living a fantasy that she'd given up on ever finding in real life. This didn't feel like a fairy tale any longer, though. She could see the way Jamie was watching her father lay Ellie down on the change table. She could feel their fear. This might be a moment that would bond a father and his unexpected daughter for ever, but it wasn't the way either of them would have chosen to bridge that gap. This was far too real to be a part of any fairy tale.

'Call Sandra if you can't find it.' Finn squeezed water from the sponge and handed it to Jamie. 'She'll know where it is.'

Hazel was pulling her phone from her pocket as she left the room. She might not need to call Sandra but she definitely needed to call Maureen and let her know she wouldn't be getting back to Two Tails any time soon. Kiara might need to come back a little earlier than she'd planned? There was no way Hazel could go back to the refuge yet.

Even increasing the distance between herself and Finn this much was hard. Hazel could feel the pull to get back to be by Finn's side as if it were an irresistible force.

The receptionist in the emergency department took one look at Finn's face as he carried the baby into the hospital, flanked by Jamie on one side and Hazel on the other, and sent them straight through to a resuscitation room to be assessed by the medical staff. He couldn't fault the response of the doctors in the department either, especially how seriously they took their examination of a sick baby.

But, as accustomed as he was to medical scenarios and procedures, this experience was overwhelming. Because he was so emotionally involved? It felt like his heart was completely exposed. Raw, even, and there was nothing he could do to protect it. Nothing that he was going to take the time to think of, anyway. He was too focused on what was going on in front of him, watching his precious Beanie get examined and listening to what the doctors were saying to each other and the questions they were asking Jamie.

'Did you have any problems with your pregnancy? Or the birth?'

'No... I didn't tell anyone for a long time, though... I...didn't have anybody.'

One of those raw bits in Finn's heart bled a little. How hard had that been for Jamie? If only he'd known...

'Temperature's thirty-nine,' a nurse reported. 'Heart rate one-eighty.'

'Respiratory rate?'

'Over fifty. Hard to count.'

'Kernig's sign?' a doctor asked.

'Negative.' Another doctor was bending the baby's legs and then she lifted her head. 'Brudzinski's sign also negative. And there's no sign of a rash.'

'Good. I'd like to get some bloods off. I'll just have a look at her ears.' The first doctor glanced up at Jamie. 'Is she up to date with her vaccinations?'

'They said she didn't need them until she was two months old.'

'Has she been unwell in the last few days? Not sleeping or feeding well?'

'I...um...'

'She's been a bit grizzly,' Finn told them. They didn't need to know that Jamie had been avoiding looking after her baby, did they? He needed to protect his daughter as well as *her* baby. Hazel had been right.

This was his family.

And…he'd been wrong in thinking he had no way of protecting his heart, because he only had to glance sideways and catch Hazel's gaze to know that he already had all the protection he needed right here beside him.

'Temperature's climbing. Thirty-nine point five. Heart rate's going up as well. One-ninety now.'

The doctors exchanged glances and one of them nodded. 'We need to rule out meningitis,' they told Jamie. 'And that means we need to do a lumbar puncture to be absolutely sure. You might want to wait somewhere else while we do that?'

It was Finn's gaze that Jamie sought. She looked terrified, even though she probably had no idea what was involved in collecting cerebral spinal fluid. She wanted his reassurance. Or maybe she just wanted to be told what she should do.

Or perhaps his daughter just needed to have him witness her taking a huge step into a new maturity.

'I'll stay with Ellie,' she said. 'I'm her mum.' But she was still holding Finn's gaze.

'I'll stay too,' he said. 'I'm Ellie's grandfather.' He'd stopped himself saying he was Jamie's father because that wasn't a relationship she wanted to claim. Or was it?

'And he's my dad,' Jamie said, tears rolling down her face as she stepped closer. 'I need him here.'

Finn held out his hand and Jamie took hold of it. Tightly.

The team were setting up rapidly to do the invasive procedure of a spinal puncture. One doctor was scrubbing his hands at a sink. A nurse was unrolling sterile packs onto the top of a trolley. There were needles there. Syringes. Small containers to collect fluid. Vials of local anaesthetic.

'I'll go and wait outside,' Hazel said.

'No…' Finn turned his head. It was Hazel's gaze he needed to catch this time. And he held out his other hand, in case she couldn't see what he was trying to communicate. 'Please don't go,' he added quietly. 'I need *you* here.'

Until the results came back and cleared baby Ellie of a serious infection that could potentially be transmissible, she was in a private room off the PICU's main corridor. On her way back from making a quick phone call to Sandra to ask her to go and check on

Ben, who had been left alone at home, Hazel found Finn standing in that corridor, looking through the internal window of Ellie's room.

The expression on his face—as if he was very close to tears—made her catch her breath and Finn must have heard that small gasp because he turned his head to watch her walk towards him. When she was just a few steps away, he held out his hand and took hold of hers.

'The results are back,' he told her. 'From the lumbar puncture and the first blood tests.'

Hazel bit her lip. She was hanging onto Finn's gaze as if her life depended on what he was about to say.

'It's nothing more serious than an ear infection,' he said quietly. 'Come in with me and let's give Jamie the good news together.'

The relief was overwhelming.

Right up there with the relief of what she'd seen in Finn's eyes earlier today, when their paths had crossed because they had both set out to find each other. Only hours ago but it felt so much longer. Too long. This was the first moment they'd actually had alone together since the moment their vehicles had been parked side by side in the driveway. Maybe that was why Hazel could feel her eyes filling with tears. Why she felt the need to hide her face for a moment in the safest place she could think of—in that hollow below Finn's collarbone—just above his heart.

And maybe that was why he let go of her hand so that he could wrap both his arms around her, so tightly it was hard to breathe, but Hazel couldn't have cared less. She needed this more than breathing. This feeling of safety. This warmth with the solid beat of Finn's heart against her cheek and the rumble of his voice so close to her ear he only needed to whisper.

'I thought I had too many things I wanted to say to you,' he said. 'But I've just figured out there's only one thing I really need to say.'

Hazel tilted her head so that she could see his face. Was it the same thing she was so desperate to tell him?

I love you...

'You're my heart, Hazel.' Finn dipped his head to brush his lips against her forehead. A soft touch that reminded her instantly of their first ever kiss. 'I love you so much that it's in every single cell in my body so it feels like that's what my heart is made of.'

Oh... That was so much better than a simple *I love you*.

It felt like the world had stopped turning. Time had stopped ticking.

Hazel's heart was so full right now it felt like it might actually burst, even though she knew perfectly well that that was a physical impossibility. It was mostly full of the love she had for Finn but that was also laced with joy. Because not only did she no longer have to hide how she felt but there were no barriers to letting it grow. And, along with that joy was an enormous amount of hope. For the future. For the happiness she knew they were going to find together. And hope was such a powerful emotion—right up there with love. And trust…

'I love you, too,' Hazel whispered, because she couldn't think of anything more poetic to say, other than that simple truth. 'I always have. I always will.'

'I think I knew that,' Finn whispered back. 'But it was too hard to trust. It was easier to pretend I couldn't see it. Or remind myself that I could never love anybody that much again. But I can. And I do… And…'

And something made him turn his head back to the window. Hazel followed the line of his gaze and saw Jamie, sitting beside Ellie's bassinet. It was obvious they were both crying. Hazel's hand found Finn's again and they were both holding on tightly as they went into the room together.

'It's okay, Jamie,' Finn said. 'Ellie's going to be fine.'

'She doesn't look fine.'

It was true that baby Ellie's face still looked red and she was making distressed snuffling sounds as she tried to cry.

'Kids are good at looking really sick,' Finn told her. 'And then they bounce back really quickly. But we know now that it's only an ear infection and not something worse. The antibiotics will kick in very soon. They're just keeping her here under observation for a bit longer to be on the safe side. I expect we'll be able to go home before too long.'

'I don't have a home,' Jamie sobbed. She reached into the bassinet to pick Ellie up. 'Neither of us do.'

'Of course you do,' Finn told her. 'You're my family and I love you. You and Beanie. And… Hazel.'

Jamie's gaze swerved to Hazel and then back to her father. 'You said you loved my mum.' There was an accusation in her tone. 'That you would never be able to love anybody else like you loved her.'

'I did say that.' Finn nodded. 'And it's still true.'

Hazel's breath caught in her throat. Hadn't he also just said that *she* was his heart?

'It was a first love with your mum,' he told Jamie softly. 'And it was the best thing that had ever happened in my life and I was completely devastated when she disappeared.' He paused to swallow hard.

'It's true,' Hazel put in. 'When he told me about your mum I knew he'd been so hurt that it made it impossible for him to trust anybody enough to love them that much. I knew how much I loved your dad but I never thought he'd be able to feel the same way.'

But he did. It was written all over his face as he watched her speaking. Hazel's heart got even more full. Maybe that was what was pushing tears up to fill her eyes yet again. The joy was overflowing.

'But…' Jamie was looking bewildered.

'Me and your mum—we were just kids,' Finn told her. 'And we *were* in love but it was an escape from the real world that we both needed. Me and Hazel? This is a grown-up kind of love. The kind that's not an escape—more like a rock that's a part of the real world. Something that's solid enough to get you through anything in life.'

Jamie was looking down at the baby she was rocking back to sleep, so they couldn't see her face but it sounded like she was still crying. 'So you get to live happily ever after, then. Like in all the fairy tales. You're lucky...'

'Real life is never a fairy tale,' Hazel said quietly. 'There's really no such thing as a happy ending because life doesn't stop. It goes on and tough things happen. But your dad's right. Love is a rock you can hang onto. So is hope.'

She looked up as she felt Finn squeeze her hand even more tightly as if he wanted to let her know he agreed and she could see that love in his eyes. She could see the same hope that she had for their future. She could also see how much he wanted to kiss her but that was going to have to wait for a more private moment than they'd managed to find in the corridor outside.

She squeezed back on Finn's hand as he turned back to his daughter.

'You're part of our lives now, Jamie. You and Beanie.'

'Am I?' Jamie finally looked up. 'But I've been horrible. Why would you want me to hang around?'

'You're family,' Finn said. 'I'm just sorry I wasn't there while you were growing up.'

'I'm sorry, too,' Jamie muttered. 'For everything.' She caught Hazel's gaze and the way she was biting her lip was an unspoken apology to her as well. 'It'll be different from now on.'

'Before and after.' Finn smiled. 'Like the two tales of Two Tails.' His smile widened. 'I've just had the best idea.'

'What?' The smile was contagious. Hazel could feel her own lips curling. Even Jamie looked like she was about to smile through the remnants of her tears although she probably had no idea what Finn was talking about.

'You know how Jude was asking if Ben was going to get his happy ending—the kind that fans of *Call the Vet* would want to see?'

'I remember...'

'What if we told his story properly? What if we told a whole bunch of stories like his? A whole series of Two Tales. A before and after. Of lives that get transformed, not just for the dogs but for the people as well?'

'I know where you could find any number of stories.' Hazel loved the idea. 'It's what Two Tails refuge is all about. And it would be wonderful because it would give people hope that, if things aren't great, they can get better. Two tales for people. Before and after. Like us. Before and after we were lucky enough to find a baby in the waiting room.' She had to kiss Finn now, despite not being alone. Just a quick kiss. A soft one. A promise of what was to come later.

'You're my after,' she whispered trying to be quiet enough to not be overheard.

'You're my for ever,' he whispered back.

'I'm here, you know,' Jamie said, with exaggerated patience. 'And I can hear you. You need to get a room, you two.' But she was definitely smiling now.

They were all smiling again a short while later, when the new set of observations on Ellie suggested that the antibiotics were already having a positive effect. Her temperature had dropped and her heart rate and breathing were back to normal. And when she woke up she wasn't grizzling at all and Jamie was able to feed a much hungrier baby.

'We're happy for you to take her home,' the doctor said.

Finn and Hazel stood up at exactly the same time. They reached for each other's hands at exactly the same time. They looked at each other and then they looked at Jamie, who had Ellie in her arms again, and Hazel could see, and feel, the one emotion that was bigger than any other in this moment.

Hope.

There was a tiny pause in the room, as if the world were holding its breath. Or maybe there was a bit of magic in the room because the pause ended with them all saying the same thing at the same time.

'Let's go home...'

EPILOGUE

Eighteen months later...

'COME ON, ELLIE...come inside, now. Grandpa's going to be on telly.'

'*No...* Soon...' The little girl with the astonishing thatch of dark curly hair was standing by the post and rail fence in front of the house, holding up single blades of grass that Isabella the donkey was taking delicately between her lips and, each time she did so, Ellie laughed.

'But Bella might be on telly, too. And Ben...'

'Ben?' Ellie turned and held up her arms to her mother. 'Where?'

'He's with Hazel.' Jamie scooped up her daughter. 'They were having a wee sleep.'

Ellie nodded solemnly. 'Hazel tired,' she said kindly. 'Bubba.'

'That's right.' Jamie carried Ellie up the

steps and into the house. 'Bubba's going to arrive any day now and that makes mum-mas tired.'

Hazel was still lying on the huge sofa in the living room but she was propped up within the circle of her husband's arm, a very contented smile on her face. The old dog with the snowy white muzzle was curled up on her other side, leaning on *her* arm. Finn pointed the remote control at the television and turned it on as Jamie sat cross-legged on the floor in front of him, tucking Ellie in for a cuddle.

'All good?' Finn glanced sideways at his daughter. 'Did you get that assignment done for uni?'

'Not quite. I'll finish it later. I'm not going to miss the very first episode of *Two Tales* going live.'

'Hmmm…' Finn sounded uncharacteristi-cally nervous. 'I'm still thinking it's going to come across as being a bit… I don't know… corny?'

They watched as the opening of the new series showed Dr Finn walking up the steps of a lovely, old cottage with a small black dog at his heels. A sign could be seen in the back-ground—*Two Tails. Please Ring and Wait.*

Finn sat down on the top step. The smile

he had for the camera had all the charm and sincerity that had made him such a star in the past. The little black spaniel that sat beside him and gazed adoringly upwards was clearly about to become a new star.

Finn fondled the dog's ears gently as he spoke. 'I've learned a lot of things in the past year or so,' he said. 'And one of them is that there are pivotal moments in life where everything can change. Points at which a story takes a breath...where a new chapter starts. And every life has its own story, doesn't it? Things change. That's another thing I've learned. It's always possible to start again.' His smile was poignant now. 'To find happiness. To find love...'

'Aww...' Hazel had to wipe her eyes.

'I know,' Finn groaned. 'I told you it was going to be corny.'

'Shh,' Jamie ordered. 'I'm listening to this.'

'I love it,' Hazel whispered. She snuggled in closer and Finn's arm tightened its hold as he dipped his head to kiss her hair.

'The stories in this series are mostly about dogs,' Dr Finn continued. 'But their stories are only part of the picture. They can only start a new chapter of their lives because of the people they meet and the lives of those people change as well. This could be seen as a series about happy endings. And it is.' He tilted his head. 'Or perhaps it isn't. It could be seen as a series about happy beginnings, instead. Anyway...' He had his hand on his companion's head now. 'This is Ben. And this is his story...'

He got up and walked down the steps, with Ben following. They walked towards pens that had other dogs in them. There was a woman working in the distance, with a girl beside her and a black and white collie nearby.

'There's Kiara,' Jamie said. 'And Bunji.' She looked up at her father. 'Bunji's getting her own story, isn't she?'

'Next episode.' Finn's face crinkled into a special smile because Ellie was also looking up at him. She held up her arms so he lifted her into his lap as the picture on the screen was blurring and then morphing into a very different scene.

A beach, a busy road, a sign that advertised the Coogee Beach Animal Hospital and then automatic doors that slid open to reveal a waiting area with a stand of dog treats and toys available for sale. Right in front of the stand was a solid, plastic pet carrier but nobody was taking any notice of it because someone was rushing through the doors. A sobbing woman.

'Please...can someone help? It just ran out in front of me...'

* * * * *

*Look out for the next story in the
Two Tails Animal Refuge duet*

A Rescue Dog to Heal Them
by Marion Lennox

*If you enjoyed this story, check
out these other great reads from
Alison Roberts*

Christmas Miracle at the Castle
Falling for the Secret Prince
Stolen Nights with the Single Dad

All available now!